I0534024

The Duchess' Necklace

Mariah Lynne

Published by
Satin Romance
An Imprint of Melange Books, LLC
White Bear Lake, MN 55110
www.satinromance.com

Cover Design by Ashley Byland from Redbird Designs

12/02-06/16

To my furry muse, Max, who loved to lay by my desk and listen endlessly to the adventures of Stormy and Duke while I wrote and rewrote *The Duchess* wagging his tail and smiling with unconditional love.

To my wonderful husband, Jerry, whose encouragement keeps me writing and my good friend Linda from Lincoln, England whose tour of Chatsworth House and lessons on English Royalty inspired the character of Amelia.

Chapter One

How dare she? How dare that woman, a common baker's wife in drab brown rags no less, speak to me with such disrespectful tones? Her whiney voice echoed in my mind long after I left her shop.

"Hope you know what a lucky lady you are, ma'am, what with all your servants and that lovely necklace. Why those emeralds and diamonds sparkle brighter than the stars in our night sky. 'Tis fit for her majesty herself." She then took her hand out of her pocket and pointed her wrinkled finger moving it so close to my jewels she almost touched them.

I took a quick step back, livid at her boldness, and left without speaking a word.

If I had a farthing for every time a commoner told me how lucky I was to be a royal, I would need a room in the manor to hold all of the coin. They tell me how they envy my servants, my sprawling estate, and my valuable family heirlooms. Why? Because they only see the good, but there is a downside, especially for an 18th century woman like myself, looking for true love.

There I sat, fourth in line for the throne, a born and bred duchess with the highest bloodlines, lonely and growing older by the minute. Men of my standing leave my bed, defiant, refusing to return. They say they found me too free spirited, too intelligent, and much too unwilling to relinquish authority to my duchy to them, even by marriage.

I realize I am not the heroine our love poets wrote about. I have the same desires as any other woman, maybe even a few more, but am left to fulfill them in secret trysts with men I wouldn't be seen with in public. One day, however, a curious set of events would change all that.

The next afternoon, I was sleeping as sound as a newborn when short, loud, popping noises shook me from a dream. *Pistol shots? Why? Who?* Startled, my heart raced. I gasped trying to catch my breath. My thoughts spun like a whirling dervish as I forced myself upright to listen for any other noises. I waited. There were none. A few minutes passed before I heard screaming female voices break the eerie silence. Frenzied chatter from outside followed before the downstairs pendulum clock chimed three times. Three in the afternoon and I'm still in bed? Peculiar. I pride myself as an early riser.

Fear caused a sudden cold draft to chill my neck. I looked down at my sheer nightshirt. Odd, it was unbuttoned down to my waist. For some unknown reason, I felt compelled to touch my neck.

My necklace! Why on earth didn't I have it on? I never take it off.

I stood rushing to my bed stand to open the top drawer. Not there. Anxious, I then combed through every inch of the bed sheets.

It's not here. Not anywhere. What will I do? My necklace is gone.

Panic left me breathless. My stomach became uneasy as I began to feel lightheaded. I slumped down into the high back chair next to the window trying to regain my composure. I hoped to remember whatever I could about where I may have left it. When I felt better, I stood and looked under my bed. I searched under the cushions of my chair. I still couldn't find it. How could I be so careless?

My necklace … my inheritance … my sole claim to my royal estate and title of duchess; how could it vanish in a flash?

My eyes flooded with tears as I remembered seeing Mr. Whitely, my Mum's private butler, at my boarding school mid-week in the throes of a winter storm. I sensed something was amiss. His dark eyes pleaded with mine. "Amelia, please accompany me home. Your mother the Duchess

2

requests it."

I tried several times on the ride back to discover why, but Mr. Whitely remained tight lipped. Once at the manor, I dashed up to my mother's bedroom only to find her pale and desperately ill. She had been my pillar of strength since we lost my father in a hunting accident. I loved her with all my heart.

Her physician by her bedside looked at me with sadness and shook his head *No*. Taking me aside, he advised, "Your Mum, Her Grace, has contracted a bitter bronchial infection. She is weak, with a high fever, and though I have tried my best to provide proper care, I see no hope for recovery. You may want to say your goodbye to her while she is still conscious. I will sit in the back of the room in case either of you needs me."

I cried collapsing in his arms. My heart was broken. She was too young to die. I was sixteen much too young to lose my mother.

I pulled myself together and walked over to her bedside. Putting on a brave smile, I kissed her forehead. She squeezed my hand. Frail as she was, she murmured something about my lineage I had not been privy to before. She told me how the king himself bestowed upon our ancestor his own neck chain to serve as a symbol in breaking the tradition of royal lineage thereby guaranteeing that whoever wore the necklace bore our ducal title and owned the estate. Because of His Highness's most generous gesture, I, a woman, could assume title ahead of my male heirs, my cousins.

Mother then whispered for me to lean over. She asked that I unclasp her necklace and hand it to her. I did so and with hands shaking, she placed the exquisite necklace around my neck. Her voice was weak but determined. "Amelia, I hereby entrust the title of Duchess of Abbington and all that it entails to you. Cherish this necklace; protect it as your standing among the other English Royal Houses depends upon it."

I gave her my word both as her daughter and now Duchess I would guard that necklace with my life. My mother, content with my promise, closed her eyes and died at peace. At that profound moment of grief, I vowed to myself never to wear my weakness on my sleeve ever again. To take charge of this duchy requires strength.

Today, however, my Mum must be tossing over in our family mausoleum. As my memory began to clear from a sleepy stupor, I remembered my affair with that cheeky scoundrel, Stuart Minton, that lying gigolo from a future time I invited back for afternoon tea. I'm quite sure he was the thief who stole my royal jewels and perhaps my future. I couldn't forgive myself, my mind still reeling at how and why I removed that chain? I always double fastened the clasps and never took my necklace off!

For the sake of a romantic tryst with a handsome stranger, I squandered my estate, broke my promise to my mother, and relinquished my place in line to the British throne all in that one reckless act. How could I be so careless? What was I thinking? Was the pleasure of my flesh more important than my duty to my title and the servants who worked the manor and farm?

If my greedy male cousins, Thaddeus and Ernest, my sole heirs to the duchy, ever find out about my missing necklace, they will be only too happy to lay claim to my inheritance and share the title. I know more than anyone how they loathe relinquishing power to a woman and still hold resentment and jealousy in their hearts because their male ancestor had been denied the necklace and thus the title for bad behavior. With no necklace in my possession, the Abbington lineage would then revert back to the eldest male of each generation.

I turned to face my bedroom doorway just as I heard the door burst open. Madeleine, my maid, rushed in. Her normally neat brown hair had fallen from its usual braided wrap. Her starched white apron stained with spots of blood. Her red eyes stared into mine as if for help. I would do anything for her—anything. She has been with me so long, I considered her family. Madeleine held up her apron to wipe her eyes. I realized then that one of my guards had been killed. I needed to know more but did not want to ask. I let her tell me.

"That awful man ..." Madeleine paused to control her sobbing. "I watched from the garden in absolute shock as Mr. Minton, that gentleman in strange attire who returned with you in your royal carriage this morning, killed young Arthur. That scoundrel shot him in the heart with one of your very own pistols. Arthur caught him trying to steal your fastest horse from the stable. Your brave young guard chased him away from the stable and down the garden path shouting, 'Stop him! Look how that man is holding on tight to his jacket. He's trying to hide something.'"

"Arthur pursued him, yelling, "'I order you to stop. Stop where you stand or I shall have to kill you.'"

"Minton paid no heed and kept going. Your brave guard drew the sword from his belt, but that dreadful man turned around and shot him. Arthur fell to the ground gasping for air. We all rushed in to assist him but he bled so furiously, we realized there was little hope for his recovery. I knelt next to him and gently raised his head to my lap. All I could do was offer comfort. Arthur gasped before pointing toward the sky. 'That man,' he said in between labored breaths, 'disappeared into thin air.' He then closed his eyes and died peacefully in my arms.

Madeleine struggled to compose herself as she wiped more tears from her eyes. I handed her one of my hankies. My mind continued to punish me. *How could I let Arthur's death happen on my watch? Why did I let my guard down and allow Minton into my life and bed only to have him steal my necklace?* Shock confused me. I needed to pull myself together in order to find that murderous scoundrel and make him pay for Arthur's death. But I knew in order to carry out my plan, my first priority must remain my necklace. Without my title, I was no help to anyone. If that murderer sold it to either Thaddeus or Ernest, before he left, my claim to the duchy was null.

I walked over to my maid and held her, desperate to console her grief.

"There, there, dear. I grieve for Arthur, as well. I promise to make this right. As long as I am the rightful Duchess of Abbington, Arthur's family will always have a home and food. I'll make sure they know this before I leave. I'll have Simon deliver my message of sympathy and support in which I tell them that Arthur was one of my most trusted guards. Madeleine, you know that I shall miss him as much as you. To honor his memory, I must leave the manor to find his killer. Now, please straighten yourself and prepare to be in charge of this manor so that I may get ready to travel."

Madeleine nodded, tears still streaming down her face. "Yes, my lady. straightaway. Will my lady be traveling far? Needing a travel bag?"

I knew I had to be careful of my answer.

"No, I cannot take one where I'm going. I will have to rely on the kindness of strangers along the way."

The tone of my voice led Madeleine to believe my method of travel was nothing extraordinary, but in fact my journey would take me to another time and a foreign place.

Madeleine curtsied and left to find a proper dress for my trip. My mind wandered, still disturbed by the recent tragedy. I realized if I were to find this murderous charlatan, I must travel to Minton's time. My personal seer, Alden, could not assist me with this. I knew I had to call on a known Traveler's friend from the future, Starr Knight, a gypsy with all the talents of a seer. Alden recommended her to me three years ago, when I lost my precious King Charles Spaniel Duke. Anxious about my journey, I walked over to my nightstand and picked up the miniature painting of Duke as a puppy. My late mother's friend, Lady Ethan, who made miniatures of all royal babies in the duchy, had painted Duke. She chided me that at her age and with my independence, she doubted if she would live long enough to see me bear a child. As I looked at his sweet face for comfort, my mind, still a bit hazy, drifted back to a certain Traveler and that most horrible day.

~ * ~

Most Travelers prove themselves to be good citizens, but a few have not been so virtuous. No matter. The Travelers I have encountered have always been a thorn in my side. Unfortunate as it was, Duke had a horrible run in with one of the devious ones.

England as well as our beloved village has long been a favorite destination for Time Travelers for all sorts of reasons. At one point, these visitors were flooding into our hamlets at such a rate the king had to put a stop to it or their numbers would destroy our quality of life. He decreed that only eight Travelers at a time would be allowed into each shire for one year's apprenticeship.

All Travelers are from future times and most anxious to learn the ways of our master jewelers, porcelain and china designers, and silversmiths so they can duplicate these skills in their own time. It seems their wealthy patrons admire the work of the English craftsmen from my time. The artisans of Abbingtonshire are well known in all of our land and beyond for their beautiful, original, and intricate designs.

All the hopefuls' names and dates of birth must be entered by their personal wizards in a lottery for all of the shires to be drawn by His Majesty's royal sorcerer.

Of course, most names drawn requested Abbingtonshire, not just for of our rolling green hills, ancient rock Roman walls, and superior craftsmen, but because we had a special offering of particular interest to them.

Once the eight names had been selected, they were sent to our local Bishop. His councilmen then questioned and approved each Traveler upon arrival before sanctioning their stay. Our council is most strict at sorting out their motives and appropriateness for study.

The Bishop of Abbington and our council hold with the highest regard their vows to provide for the poorest in our hamlet. Several years ago, our local council by formal proclamation decreed that Travelers shall be provided room and board in the church annex, as well as guaranteed apprenticeships with our best tradesmen in whatever field they so choose. It is well known that our craftsmen are the best in all of England, but what truly separates us from the other hamlets in a Traveler's eye is this generous welcome endowment.

Once approved, Travelers must honor our good will by swearing to a secret arrangement where they shall bring us ten pounds of sterling along with a donation of goods and crafts in their own field from their time. These coins and gifts are either given to our poorest citizens directly or placed in a holiday sale which proceeds assist our poorer residents.

The incoming Travelers must first be sworn to secrecy by their seers; their pledges bound in writing then sent to The Bishop of Abbington who places his holy seal upon the document. In the past, they have brought bedding, cookware, clocks, as well as tins of delicious chocolates, cookies and toys for the children. The Travelers are pleased to donate and enjoy celebrating the holiday with us at Abbington Cathedral decked out in its holiday greenery and yule candles for our Carol Service.

Because of this secret exchange, our hamlet parish now believes it has the richest alms for the poor fund in all of England. It even assists our farmers and non- skilled laborers.

The other church councils still scoff at us advising that accommodating Travelers in such a generous manner depletes our hamlet's reserves and is a guaranteed way to lose church funds and raise tithes. But since they are not aware of our secret pact, they have no idea how much money our special program truly brings in. We intend to keep it that way. Our funds are so great that the church vestries can negate the tithing of locals offering full apprenticeships and reduce those of the other residents. Of course, townspeople are notified yearly of all Travelers serving as apprentices and always try to keep a watchful eye on them to guarantee they do not abuse the rules of their stay.

~ * ~

I'm afraid my guard, Edward, was not so diligent on that fateful day and because of that, I experienced heartache like never before. Duke was a very special pup, not just because he was mine, but because our king gave him to me from his own dog's litter. Black and tan, Duke caught the eye of every dog fancier. Aware of their interest, I kept a tight watch over him. I smiled, remembering I named him Duke because I never romanced a man with whom I wished to share my title.

Duke was playing in his private fenced in garden as unbeknownst to me a known time Traveler to our village watched from a nearby stonewall. At any rate, my guard, Edmund, whom I sent to protect Duke, rushed inside the manor house, breathless. He ran in and out of the drawing room and dining room before he found me in the library reading. When I noticed Duke was not with him, I stood, hands trembling in fear that something awful had happened.

My guard hesitated before speaking these dreadful words. "My Grace. Please forgive me. I'm sad to report that our Duke has been taken. I watched that beautiful pup chase his ball around until Jerome called for me go to the stable to look at one of your horse's hooves. Jerome was having trouble replacing it. I helped him and was gone but a few minutes. In that short time span, a known Traveler who had been watching him at play, must have jumped into Duke's yard and grabbed him. I raced back to the yard when I saw Duke in his arms and shouted for him to halt or I would shoot him, but the thief vanished in an instant into thin air right before my eyes."

I was speechless. When Edmund told me that my Duke was missing, my heart shattered into tiny pieces. I was devastated and couldn't bear the thought of living without my precious pet. I wiped my tears, ordering Edmund to go into the village center to find out what he could about this heartless thief. Prior to this day, no one had reported this Traveler as devious. I hoped he would ask for a ransom. I would pay dearly but alas that was not to be.

I paced the library floor crying my eyes out. I would do anything to get my Duke back. My guard returned later that day to report the local tavern owner had informed him this Traveler mentioned, after a few too many ales, that he was a breeder of King Charles Spaniels from the time of 2010. He was searching for one with the purest bloodline to take back to his time for breeding. There were none purer than my Duke unless he stole the king's own dog.

I continued to weep, fearful that my little Duke was gone forever. I called for Madeleine and asked her to find my personal seer, Alden.

"Please ask Alden to come immediately. Tell him it's urgent. Tell him a Traveler took my Duke, and I need Alden's guidance to find him.

Hurry, Madeleine. Please hurry!"

It was not very long before Madeleine returned with Alden. Just seeing my kind old seer gave me strength. Alden had long fine white hair and a long gray beard. He limped over to me using a walking stick. He stopped and took my hand as he looked into my eyes with his sympathetic ones.

"Amelia. I have not visited with you in years and am happy to see you even though these are not happy times. You are under extreme duress which I hope to relieve. Odd, I had a premonition before Madeleine came for me that Duke had been taken. Unfortunately, I cannot help you find him, but am able to connect you to someone who can. Her name is Starr Knight, a skilled seer and gypsy in the time of 2010. I know this is not what you want to hear, but in order to find Duke; you must travel to that thief's time."

"I have already contacted Starr on your behalf as soon as Madeleine confirmed my suspicions about Duke's disappearance. If you truly wish to find your pup, you must follow the directions Starr Knight sent me. Please trust me and trust her. She has the special talents you need to locate your lost dog. Do not deviate, trick, or lie. Her powers are greater than they seem."

I trusted Alden with all my heart so I decided to Travel to meet Starr. Anxious about what I had to do, I looked deep into Alden's dark brown eyes.

"You know I trust you more than anyone. I have since I was a young girl. I will do anything you ask of me to get my loving dog back."

Alden nodded, looking pleased by my answer.

"Amelia, in most cases, Starr said that it could take up to three hours for her to hear your plea and send help, but because of my past contacts with her, she awaits your call. On my honor, I asked her to promise me to help you now and any time in the future you find yourself needing her assistance. She gave me her word as a fellow seer that she would. Now, please stand over here and face that painting."

Of course I did what my trusted seer said. He positioned me with my back against the wall while facing the opposite wall that held the large painting of my manor gardens. Shaking, I stood there waiting for further instruction.

"Amelia, you must now call out to Starr, stating her name three times with 'present' after each call."

I understood I had no choice but to do as he said. "Starr present."

I stood straight against the wall, not knowing what to expect next. I called out to her again and again. "Starr present. Starr present. Starr present."

My stomach felt unsettled as I waited to see what would happen next. Finally, I turned when I heard a whisper of a sound as soft winds entered the room. They were the winds of time strengthening as they approached. Without warning, they picked me up and swirled me around. Their robust gusts blew the window open before lifting me through it high into the clouds. I was deathly afraid to open my eyes for fear of falling. After I calmed down, I spread my arms out wide, drifting back and forth like a hawk in flight. I felt a bit dizzy before the winds dropped me all too suddenly in a corner of what I came to know as Starr's front yard.

Lucky for me, she was starting a flowerbed and had just placed a fresh mound of soil right where I landed. That made for a much softer landing than I anticipated. I stood and shook the topsoil from my garments before looking around. The air was much warmer than I was accustomed. Stifling, I stopped to unbutton the top of my blouse. It was night and lucky for me no one was nearby to see.

I was well aware I could not spare another minute. I was on a mission to save my baby. I headed straight to the front steps of the house. I stopped when I saw the gypsy's sign:

STARR E. KNIGHT
SEEKER OF LOST PETS
FINDER OF TRUE LOVE AND HAPPY DREAMS

That was precisely why I was here. I ran up the green wooden steps and knocked on her front door's stained glass window. It was a few minutes before she answered, but those minutes seemed like hours. Starr opened the door. I looked into her kind eyes.

There she stood. Nothing like I imagined. No fancy robes of a seer, no amulet or magic wand. She was dressed like a peasant in light colored sequined fabric of rose and lavender. Her skirt was much shorter than proper length for a lady while her long hair was tied back in a blue scarf. I looked up into the most caring eyes I'd ever seen. She took my hand and escorted me inside.

"Amelia, Alden relayed the message about a Traveler taking Duke from you. You must be devastated. Please come into my reading room and make yourself comfortable."

She escorted me down a short hallway before entering a pleasant looking room. I walked over to a large round table covered with a blush lace tablecloth. I peered around the pale pink room, looking at all the pictures of happy couples dressed in wedding regalia on her wall and all the cats and dogs with their smiling owners. Oh, how I hoped her next picture would be of Duke and me. Starr pointed to a chair.

"Please sit down here next to me, and I promise I'll see what I can find out." A pitcher with two glasses was on a tray next to her. Starr filled the glasses.

"Try some of our sweet Southern iced tea. You must be parched. Time Travel can be so exhausting!"

I was thirsty indeed and took a sip as I watched her turn around. She opened the bottom of the mirrored sideboard behind her. She took something solid out and placed it on the table in front of her. At first, I paid no attention. I was so dry and the chilled tea so delicious, I gulped down the rest of the glass before I saw what it was. There, right in front of my eyes, stood a most exquisite pink crystal ball. Any of the seers in my duchy would have vied for such an article of pure beauty. Starr glanced over at me, moving one finger over her mouth to indicate I should be quiet. I couldn't talk since I was taken aback by a soft cherry glow coming from the center of her crystal ball. Waving her slender fingers around the ball, Starr closed her eyes and spoke Duke's name slowly with conviction.

"Duke … Duke … Duke … Show me where you are. Your mistress Amelia is worried about you. She misses you. Duke my puppy, reveal to us where to find you. Amelia wants to bring you home."

As soon as she finished, colored lights in different shades of pink and blue exploded from her crystal ball circling the walls. They mesmerized me as Starr kept working her magic. The lights flickered before they stopped. Starr gasped.

Chapter Two

"Look! There he is! I found him! He's very cute. No wonder you love him so much. By the sad look in his eyes, I bet he misses you as well. He must have escaped his dog-napper because he's in a shelter right outside of Washington, D.C."

Starr's words lost me completely. Tears streamed down my cheeks.

"Kind lady, you speak gibberish. What is a shelter? Where is Washington, D.C.?"

The gypsy touched my hand.

"Amelia please trust me. Washington is our nation's capital city. A shelter houses lost or abandoned animals."

I blurted out. "Duke was neither abandoned nor lost. He was taken."

"I know, but evidently he is as feisty and independent as I was told you are. I can see how he jumped out of his dog napper's arms and outran him down the road only to be found much later by a kind Samaritan who brought him to the shelter. Now, you must brace yourself because I am going to ask you to Travel again. You are in Florida, a city called Ft. Myers, to be precise. I need to send you to Washington where Duke is. You cannot leave now because it is eight o'clock at night and the animal shelter that houses him is closed until morning."

"But first I will send you upstairs where you can wash and get a good night's rest. In the morning, you must change your clothes to

14

appear that you are from this time. Please go into my guest room which is right at the top of the stairs. We are about the same size. I will select an outfit for you from my closet. Tomorrow morning, when you are ready, come back down to Travel again. Will you be all right with that?"

I nodded. After all, what choice did I have? I dragged my tired body up the twelve stairs to do what she'd asked. I washed myself in her tub filled with peculiar water that needed no boiling, before getting undressed and ready for bed. Starr knocked on my door.

"Amelia, your clothes are ready. May I bring them in?'"

Answering yes, she came in and hung them on the open closet door. I slept like a baby that night knowing that she would help me. The first rays of morning sun awoke me from my dream of holding my Duke again. I dressed in a blue skirt and blouse quickly and went downstairs ready and resolute to travel. Starr was having tea.

"Care for a cup and some toast?"

"No. I am not very hungry. I just want to find my dog."

She understood and instructed me as Alden did previously to stand against the wall but this time to face an open window. The gypsy spoke in a soft serious tone.

"Amelia, your problem should be resolved, but bear in mind my skills are limited by cosmic rules. Once you travel, you cannot take longer than seven days, or you will turn into your real age in my time or dust. I will not be able to reverse that. If you run into problems, contact me as you did before. Now, when you are ready to go get Duke, repeat what I say three times. 'Starr, take me to Duke.'"

Of course I did as she said. When I finished the last call, the winds of time were quick and entered through the open window. They picked me up and carried me up and out. Not as frightened, I rather enjoyed being as light as a cloud floating through the air over trees and small mountains until thud …

I fell, hitting the ground hard right in front of a sign that read: COUNTY ANIMAL SHELTER. I jumped up and brushed the travel dust from my clothes. I looked at the large one floor sprawling building as I heard dogs barking. One sounded like my own dog's whimper. Racing inside, I called for Duke by name.

"Duke, my little laddie. I know you're here. Bark again to direct me."

Just as I finished, a lady in a red striped uniform jumped up from her chair behind an old wooden desk near the front entrance. The sign on her desk read "Receptionist. All visitors must stop here." Well, I wasn't about to stop not when it came to getting my Duke back. I plowed by her desk when she stood in front of me. I stopped short not wanting to hurt her. She looked at me with a bit of disdain.

"Why the hurry? I'm here to help you. Now tell me, are you here to adopt an animal or to find a lost one?"

I couldn't control my feelings and started to cry.

"My little Duke. I need to find my dog. He means everything to me."

Her eyes softened and she took my hand.

"Miss, please take it easy. My name is Kathleen Kemp and I am the receptionist. I will do everything in my power to reunite you with your dog. I heard your calls from inside. You say his name is Duke. When they are rescued we don't know their original name unless it's on their collar. Tell me everything you can about him and where you thought he was lost so I can see if one matches his description. Unfortunately, we have many dogs in here at the present time."

I caught my breath. "Someone stole my dog right out of my fenced yard. I do live quite far from here, but a good friend said she did see him in here. He's a King Charles Spaniel, black and tan, and answers to 'Duke,'" I replied.

"Duke, of course. I do believe we did have one matching your description that was turned in two days ago. I believe he's still here. Let me take you to his pen."

This kind lady led me by so many cages of homeless dogs. I looked into their sad eyes wishing I could help them all. The shelter was damp and the cages small with hard floors and small windows where they could go outside. Certainly, not proper for a dog of Duke's royal bloodlines. I felt sorry for them. Royal or not, it wasn't right for any of them, but their stay here might help their owners locate them. I would take them all home to my manor if I could. I smiled thinking that might be a bit difficult for Starr to manage. We stopped at one pen where Miss Kathleen thought Duke was being held. We were surprised to find the door open and Duke nowhere in sight. My heart sank like an anchor. Tears streamed down my cheeks. Kathleen stopped a young man wearing a red vest with "Shelter Staff" printed on it.

"Excuse me, Mike, do you know where the King Charles Spaniel we named Spunky is?"

"Yeah. As a matter a fact, I just saw him in the pre-adoption room playing with a well-dressed man. The man seemed interested in him. Hopefully, Spunky will find a great new home. He's a fun dog!"

I became frantic upon hearing the news. I couldn't help but blurt out. "Spunky? That's not Spunky. That's my Duke. There'll be no great new home for him. Not as long as I have breath. Now, hurry please, take me to him. I must get Duke back before another scoundrel takes off with him!"

I could sense Kathleen was more than a bit taken back by my response. She briskly walked me to a large open room where a few people were playing with dogs. My eyes scanned the room until I shouted out.

"There he is. I see him! Oh Duke! Duke, come here, baby!"

I spotted Duke in the arms of a tall lanky gentleman. The dog did not seem bothered by the fact a total stranger held him. Actually, he seemed to enjoy it. I noticed the man's hair was blond with just a touch of gray. Standing with his back to me, he held Duke on his shoulder scratching his little head. The man had a solid build. Before I could observe any further, Duke spotted me, bolted out of the man's arms, and

17

raced over. I gladly picked him up, closed my eyes, and hugged him as tight as I could before I became distracted by the fresh scent of pine surrounding me. When I opened my eyes, that quite handsome gentleman was standing directly in front of me. Even with spectacles, his clear blue eyes took mine hostage. He hesitated for a few minutes to speak. He may be the shyest man I ever met. He took a deep breath before engaging in conversation. "Excuse me, Ma'am. I'd like to introduce myself. My name is Ryan Redstone."

My eyes delighted on him as my romantic mind wouldn't stop spinning. Ryan Redstone, what a delicious name.

We chatted for a short time. I would have enjoyed more, but I knew I had no choice but to leave him if I wanted to get my Duke home in safety. I waited for Ryan to leave the room before walking over to a quiet corner hidden from the view of the other patrons. With Duke in my arms, while reluctant to leave the man I just met, I was cognizant of my time restraints; I called out for Starr to take us home.

The winds of time arrived as fast as a flash of lightning. They carried us home in the most gentle of cool breezes. I covered little Duke's eyes so he wouldn't be afraid of flying so high up in the sky. He licked my face as I thought that Ryan, oddly enough, was the first man Duke liked. Duke and I must have the same taste because I found it difficult to get Ryan out of my mind and hadn't been able to since.

~ * ~

My mind snapped back to the present when I heard Madeline return with my clothes.

"My lady, are you all right?"

"Yes. Just deep in thought. Sorry."

"No need to apologize. You carry the weight of our duchy on your shoulders."

Madeleine sighed as she helped me dress in a proper two piece velvet ensemble. She had to stop every few minutes to wipe the tears in her eyes.

18

"You know, my Grace, that Arthur was just a bit older than my own boy. He was a treasure and I shall miss him dearly."

She turned ready to leave me alone to finish my personal travel preparations, but I had two requests before she left.

"Madeleine, please summon Simon and tell him to come here. He always took Arthur under his wing, and I need his help in notifying Arthur's family. Also, take extra good care of my little Duke."

Madeleine smiled and curtseyed. She knew I wanted to do the right thing by Arthur and how much I loved that little dog.

"Yes, My Lady, will do both. Now don't you worry."

I went to my writing desk, took out stationery with my royal seal, and inked my quill pen. I wrote about my thoughts of Arthur adding sympathy for his family and my pledge to take care of whatever they needed. Just as I finished I heard a solid knock on my door. It was Simon, my senior guard, who was strong physically and emotionally. He arrived promptly after Madeleine's request. I tried to control my feelings of grief, but my eyes streamed tears at just the thought of Arthur's bravery on my behalf. I pulled myself together to address my guard.

"Simon, I have written a message of sympathy for you to deliver to Arthur's family. I know you were his closest confidant among my guards and that he held you with fatherly esteem. Please tell them I cannot visit at this time as I have deemed it my mission to bring his killer to justice. I am sure you will miss him as much as I."

Simon nodded in acknowledgement. I then folded my note and placed it in an envelope bearing my royal seal before handing it to him. His sad eyes said it all.

"Thank you, Ma'am. I know Arthur would have appreciated your thoughtful words. He always told me how proud he was to serve in your guard."

With that, Simon bowed and left. At that point, I knew I had to get down to the business of my missing necklace. I remembered what the gypsy instructed me to do. She herself admitted it could take as long as

19

three hours for the winds of time to reach me so I began the process at once. Looking out my window up at the sky, I called out, "Starr future! Starr future! Starr future!"

While I waited, I finished my preparations slipping a velvet pouch into my bodice. I opened my dresser drawer and removed a special drawing, folded it, and placed it in my skirt pocket along with a lavender lace fan. Once I completed that task, I placed another important item deep into my other pocket. My timing was impeccable. As soon as I took my hand out, I began to hear those eerie sounds of the winds of time as they approached.

With the speed of a gazelle, those winds entered my room wrapped me in their continuous whirlwind until … whoosh! They picked me up and swirled me around the inside of the cyclone. Out the open window we flew. I looked down at my manor house. It looked like a palace miniature as I raced through the clouds. Then suddenly … crash! I landed much harder than I had hoped. Oh, how I wished there was an easier way for a lady of my standing to Travel. I looked around. Yes, perfect aim. I had landed directly on Starr's front lawn. As a matter of fact, I faced that familiar sign near her entrance. A bit of a marvel, that. I was relieved to read the pink pastel tubes of light once more:

STARR E. KNIGHT
SEEKER OF LOST PETS
FINDER OF TRUE LOVE AND HAPPY DREAMS

Straightening, I turned when I heard Starr's nosey neighbor shout from across the street.

"Hey Susie, did you hear that?"

I glared at the man. He appeared older with gray hair and was leaning over the front railing of his porch staring at me through a pair of field glasses. Probably never saw a proper royal before. This annoying commoner kept talking, much to my dismay.

"Susie, do you see that lady over there?"

He fanned himself with folded papers; I'm quite sure trying to attract any breeze he could. It felt quite warm for a spring evening. Susie, the woman I assumed to be his wife, was dressed in man's trousers and a light shirt. She put down her book to take a solid look at me, as well.

"Well, Herb, what do you know?" she answered. "It's amazing that woman doesn't suffocate with that long velvet outfit on. Gotta be in the eighties out here tonight. I bet she's with that medieval festival at the river park. Starr sure does attract some strange ones. Oh, oh, turn around. That woman's looking over here at us. Pretend you're asleep. Don't need any of Starr's crazies bothering us."

Crazies! Imagine the nerve of that woman calling me a crazy. Amelia Augusta Ethrington, the Duchess of Abbington, fourth in line to the throne, a crazy. Why, that woman would be locked up and sent to the stockade for less at home. Her husband sat back down and pulled his cap forward to cover his eyes while she closed hers and rested her head back against her rocking chair. I ignored them. I knew I had more important matters that needed attending.

Brushing the travel dust off my purple velvet skirt and bodice, I marched up to Starr's front door. Pounding on it as hard as I could, I shouted, "Starr! Open this door now! I order you by royal decree. You swore to Alden when I lost Duke that you would help me with any other problem I had in the future. I now have a big one only your skills are able to resolve."

No answer. How dare that gypsy ignore me! Frustrated, I burst into tears. No one ignores me. I called out and pounded again.

"Starr, answer this door now! I shall continue to shout until you do. Your neighbors across the path appear intrigued by me. Maybe I should tell them how I arrived here? Hurry. I'm melting in this dress. I haven't ever felt this hot."

I looked up at her stained glass window on the front door. I heard footsteps and saw her figure approach through the blue crinkled glass with a yellow crescent moon and gold stars embellished on it. Finally, I heard her heavy wooden door creak open. Starr wearing a stained green

21

gingham apron looked more than a bit surprised to see me.

"Why, Amelia, what on earth are you doing here now? Are you all right? You look anxious. Oh my, I must not have been paying attention to the right time. I was not expecting you for at least two more hours. I'm so sorry. I kept track of your journey on my kitchen clock. It must have stopped while I was mixing a potion for another client's spell. I must get that clock fixed. Please forgive my carelessness. Nevertheless, it's wonderful to see you again."

The gypsy looked deep into my reddened eyes as I spoke.

"Starr, you more than anyone can understand the urgency of my visit. I'm on the brink of losing my duchy. Desperate and despondent, I seek your help once more."

Starr's eyes darted across the street. Noticing her neighbors' continued interest, she pulled me inside, quickly trying to calm my frazzled nerves.

"Amelia, please go into my reading room before you die of heat. The air's the coldest in there. Make yourself at home. You've been here before. I'll get us some chilled tea."

I never had chilled tea until I visited Starr … peculiar but refreshing. I walked into her reading room, collapsing on the first chair I saw. The breeze from the large rattan ceiling fan felt good, but was not enough to cool me down. I took my lace fan from my pocket and fanned myself. Once cool, I removed the folded piece of paper from that same pocket and placed it on the table.

Starr returned without the apron but with a pitcher of chilled tea and some lemon, sugar, two glasses, and long spoons. She poured the tea.

"What could be so bad that can't be fixed? I heard from another with the gift that you fell head over heels for a Traveler. I heard he was young and very handsome." Starr winked. "And that he was a wealthy merchant of antiques and reproductions."

I nodded. "Aye, he was a handsome lad, all right. Too handsome. In love? I don't think so. He was just a dalliance. By the way, he wasn't a wealthy merchant of antiques, but a scoundrel of the lowest kind ... an unscrupulous Traveler like the one who stole Duke, out to see what he could steal and bring to his own time for profit. I called you for help since his time is the same as yours. You know I'll pay you. I'm good for it."

To prove my point, I pulled the small black velvet pouch from my bodice. I saw Starr's eyes widen as I emptied fifty small gold pieces onto the table. *Aha! By the look in her eyes, I know I have her attention. Once a gypsy always a gypsy.*

After I emptied the pouch, I pushed as many gold pieces as I could grasp over to Starr. She appeared surprised by how much I intended to pay her. She picked up a couple of the coins, feeling the gold in her hand before looking at me.

"So much? My old friend, I cannot accept all of this. It's too much."

I sat back and smiled. "It's meager compared to my duchy. Besides, I would refrain from judgment on your price until you hear what I need you to do. It's tricky even for someone as gifted as you."

Starr was eager to hear more.

"Tricky, huh? Well, I haven't had one of those in a while. Here, have another sip of tea before you tell me everything from the beginning."

Starr poured some more of the chilled tea for both of us. After taking a quick sip, I gulped down the entire glass. Very unladylike. Starr appeared surprised by my thirst so I thought I must explain.

"As you well know, Time Travel can deplete a lady of fluids."

Looking into the gypsy's dark eyes, I began. "What I am about to tell you, my sister, is serious business. It involves a seer, a necklace, and a handsome young lover with a promise that wasn't kept."

Starr leaned forward, intent on listening to my every word. She smirked. "I know you like your lovers young, but how young was he? My, my, Amelia, you sure do know how to attract them."

I lifted my chin, annoyed by Starr's attempt at humor. "You have no idea how hard it is for an older woman of thirty-two to find a young, artful lover. Most feel I am past their point of interest."

Starr laughed. "Thirty-two. Ah, to be that young again. Please, I'll be quiet. Start from the beginning. I have two hours until my next client."

After moving the piece of paper I had placed on the table closer to us, I grabbed my neck for something that wasn't there.

"Oh Starr, you are the most trusted among us Travelers. I know I should have known better, but his kisses were so sweet, filled with such passion, while his caresses so tender. I couldn't control my lust, my deepest desires."

Starr had to interrupt. "You're skipping over one important detail. Who is he?"

The mere thought of that man's skills as a lover made me flush with excitement. "I guess I'm a bit ahead of myself. That's what a passionate man will do to you. His name is Stuart Minton. A Traveler, he claimed to be in his mid- twenties. His age did not matter only his muscular build and penetrating dark brown eyes. He had light brown wavy hair. Oh, you know the kind you'd like to run your fingers through."

"We ran into each other by chance or so I thought at the time inside the bakery shop. I now know he most likely waited for me since I frequent the shop daily. At any rate, he bowed like a proper gentleman and introduced himself. He asked if he could walk with me back to my manor. Since he spoke with a certain degree of intelligence and looked so delicious, I agreed."

Starr smirked.

"A delicious stranger? Why not am I not surprised?"

I was not amused by that and wanted to shoot her a glare of disdain but refrained because of my necklace.

"May I continue? As we chatted, Minton represented himself as a student craftsman wishing to learn the techniques of the master jewelers of my time. I know I should have required proper documentation before taking his request seriously, but with a name like Minton, I wrongly assumed him to be a future relative of the Earl Nathaniel Minton, a neighbor of sorts. Our estates adjoin one another's. Sadly, I never checked."

Embarrassed, I gestured with my hand.

"Minton further stated that there was intense interest from the well-to-do ladies of your time for replicas of our jewelry. Being a lover of jewels myself, his request intrigued me—not to mention his sexual appeal."

"Minton then further revealed that he was a jeweler by trade coming from the time of 2013 He procured a seer to send him directly to me. In researching the jewelry of my time, he found my craftsmen the most artistic in all of England. At first, I thought him peculiar, but having known of other Travelers wishing to study artisans in my duchy, I accepted his story as true. He asked if I would take him to our local shops and introduce him to the jewelers."

Starr appeared entranced by my story so to illustrate I turned my head and lifted my hair to better show my ruby and sapphire drop earrings set in gold. I did like how the gold and glitter set off my chestnut brown tresses.

"As you can see, my jewelers are brilliant, I might add." Starr reached over and held one of the earrings in her hand. "Beautiful workmanship. So intricate. They are just exquisite."

I beamed at her admiration. "My jewelers are the very best. Renowned for their fine gold work, both of my master jewelers are transplanted from Florence. Anyway, I sent a guard to make appointments for him to work with the jewelers the next day and asked that he meet me outside the bakery shop. He agreed and after we met, I took him inside to meet both of them, as well as their apprentices. I sent a guard to make appointments for him to work with the jewelers the next day."

A note of shame colored my voice. "Once we completed our visits, I invited him to share my carriage back to my manor. After all, I am the Grand Duchess of Abbington.

"As soon as we arrived, I invited him in for tea as any good hostess would do. I escorted him through the grand foyer into my main drawing room. As we walked around the manor house, I noticed how large his eyes grew at its opulence. The tall blue and white Chinese vases filled with feathers greeted our entrance to the sitting room. I escorted him to the large garnet velvet settee and instructed him to sit down."

"Since it was late morning, I rang for my maid Anne. Dressed in the pink and grey uniform of the manor staff, I asked her to bring us some Earl Grey tea and butter biscuits with jam. I hoped that would ease conversation about the jewelry and art from his time. My maid obliged, leaving the door open behind her. Duke snuck in, ran over to Minton, and tried to bite him. I realize now that I should have paid stricter attention to his growling. Instead, I called for Anne to take him out of the room."

I glanced skyward, gathering strength to admit my indiscretion.

"Minton told me in the course of his research, he came across a famous necklace, The Abbington Jewels. He proceeded to describe my yellow diamond and emerald necklace. He asked if his research proved correct. Of course, I nodded yes before he asked if there was any way he could see it."

Starr interrupted me. "Is this the necklace Alden contacted me about?"

I puzzled. "Alden? How could he know? I told no one except my most trusted maid."

Starr touched my hand. "Do not be afraid. You should know your secret is safe with him. Alden loves you as much as if you were his own daughter. He keeps a watchful eye on you since your parents' deaths and would never betray you. He sent me a message from his crystal ball, which I might add, is much more powerful than mine. He told me that when he looked into his crystal ball hoping to find a recipe for a potion to cure a sick neighbor, he witnessed a thief with your necklace under his jacket leaving your manor and calling his seer to assist his Travel through time. Alden, more than anyone, knows what turmoil would come to your duchy and sent me a message at once to ask for my assistance. His message preceded your call. Now please confirm that this is the same necklace?"

Distressed, I shook my head affirmative.

"My necklace bears a royal honor like no other set of jewels in England. Because of that, there has been as much ill will surrounding that necklace as beauty. 'Tis absolutely shameful to have such venomous animosity between family members over those jewels. Imagine, this royal blood feud continues to my time."

Starr appeared eager to learn more.

"A blood feud? How awful. How did it start?"

I paused to gather my thoughts.

"One hundred years ago, my great-great-great uncle, Duke Hestor of Abbington, fell gravely ill. Hestor was a large strapping man who became weak, had difficulty breathing, and dizzy. His royal physician advised him to put his papers in proper order because he was facing death. Duke Hestor, while most concerned about his illness, felt just as troubled about the future of his duchy. As he began to write his will, the duke recognized he needed help if he were to secure his duchy's future."

"The duke sired two children. His son, George, the eldest of the siblings, was a dashing lad who had a penchant for gambling, women of the evening, and drink. George cared little about his own conduct since he felt entitled, being both male and the eldest child. The duke, now helpless, watched George squander his money and sell the duke's most prized possessions. The reckless young royal even killed a commoner over a woman in a pub fight in the village. Hestor knew George would destroy the family's royal honor and could lose the title."

"On the other hand, Hestor's daughter, Susanne, always made him proud. She was not only beautiful but bright, caring, and cultured, both

27

in the arts and social graces. She visited him daily, reading poems to him every night on his sick bed. The duke knew Susanne would be the better choice to succeed him but wondered how he could upend royal tradition. He needed the assistance of a higher source."

"That night after his doctor's sad news, Hestor removed some paper and an envelope from his bed stand and began to write the note he hoped would change the future of his duchy. The next morning, Duke Hestor summoned his most trusted guard, Peter, and asked him to visit King Charles to ask a favor for a dying duke. He handed Peter the envelope addressed to His Majesty Only. The guard followed Hestor's instructions and rode hard and fast to deliver the letter to the king. Of course, King Charles was surprised to see Hestor's guard in his court. Charles called the guard forward and proceeded to read the letter at once. The king expressed his concern to Peter about Hestor's deteriorating condition. His Majesty was fond of the duke and realized he owed Hestor, since the duke was one of a handful of royals who remained loyal to the monarch in a past uprising. The king called for his carriage and royal guard without delay."

"Not residing far from Abbington Manor, His Majesty rode a mere half day to visit the dying duke. When King Charles entered Hestor's room, the ailing duke wanted to stand from his sickbed and show his proper respect. He tried but fell back in bed. His Majesty motioned for the ailing duke to stay put."

"'Hestor, please remain in bed. I know I have your respect. You have been a most loyal supporter. I want you to know that I read your letter as soon as it was delivered and am as troubled by your dilemma as you. Your decision would break all royal tradition. Tell me why this is necessary, and if I deem it proper, I will find a way to make it happen.'"

"Hestor moaned before pouring his heart out to the king about George, who listened as a brother rather than a monarch. When Hestor finished, King Charles spoke."

"'Hestor, George would wreak havoc upon your dukedom which easily could transcend to my reign. Even though a daughter may only succeed you if you have no sons and add that 'tis unheard of for a royal to choose his successor, I believe in your case you have just cause.'"

"The King wore a heavy rope of gold chain, laced with yellow diamonds and emeralds. As he spoke, he removed it from around his neck."

"'I will issue a royal decree stating Susanne will succeed you as Duchess of Abbington Manor. The decree is for this one time only and may pass to her heirs. However, if Susanne or any of her descendants break the law, or manages to lose or damage this chain of royal lineage I am about to present, the duchy reverts back to George or his heirs. One copy of the decree will stay with me in the royal palace; the other will be brought here to post on the wall of Abbington Manor.'"

"'This heavy rope of gold is my favorite, given to me on my twentieth birthday by its owner, my grandmother, the queen. I wore it under my uniform in battle and believe it brought me much luck. I only hope, my trusted friend, it does the same for your family. The necklace may be worn by either a man or a woman, and shall serve as a crown for the royal title of the Duchy of Abbington. As I place this around your neck, I decree this in front of my guards in the year of our Lord 1661.'"

"King Charles then placed the chain of royal lineage around Hestor's neck before continuing."

"'My royal seal is on the underside of the clasp. Now, go in peace, my loyal friend. You may choose your successor with an easy heart.'"

"With that, the king touched Hestor's hand and left, preceded by his guards.

"The duke, tears of gratitude streaming down his cheeks, called for both of his children. He announced that he chose Susanne, my great-great grandmother, as his successor. George was furious, vowing revenge until his dying day. My two greedy cousins are George's direct descendants. Either of those two unruly earls, Thaddeus or Ernest, could be George reincarnated. They behave like the bad marionettes in a Punch and Judy show."

I laughed. "They are awkward and stiff and move like they are

29

attached to strings when they are together. They would be more than happy to steal my necklace given any opportunity and have even tried. They attempt to wreak havoc by bursting into my manor unannounced, trying to frighten my servants into giving them the jewels. So far, they have been unsuccessful, but now with the necklace stolen, I must watch my back every minute. I know Minton stole it, but I'm quite sure for the right price, the young earls could purchase it from that unscrupulous thief. I cannot confide that my necklace is missing to the King. He would have to follow the laws of royal inheritance and invoke the original proclamation in which the duchy would immediately revert back to the next male in line. How could I have let my defenses down to a total stranger?"

Starr tried her best to console me. "We all have our failings. Please tell me more about Mr. Minton."

I took a deep breath before continuing. Just the thought of that scoundrel made my blood boil.

"At the time, I actually thought little of his request to see the necklace. I had it on under my bodice. I used to wear it in plain view until I tired of all the envy let alone the fear that it might be ripped off my neck. Now I show it only in the company of those of similar standing. That afternoon, I'm sad to say desire overtook my common sense."

I folded my hands on my lap. "I offered to show it to him—at the proper time of course. After all, I wear it, or should say wore it daily. We have been blessed with privilege, but come from a long line of soldiers and men of the cloth."

Starr touched my sleeve. "You should be proud."

I nodded, acknowledging her kind statement before continuing.

"Minton appeared most interested in, not only the necklace, but me, so after tea I invited him into my private drawing room for a glass of sipping sherry as any proper hostess would do. He began to flaunt his charm at me as soon as we entered the room. He complemented me on my choice of furniture and told me he liked how the colors accentuated my complexion."

"Any older woman in her right mind would love hearing compliments such as his. I led him to the royal blue silk brocade settee and invited him to sit next to me. Once seated, Minton soon leaned over and whispered in my ear, rather naughtily, I might add, that he would love seeing such a beautiful lady as I, wearing that necklace and nothing else. Of course, I harrumphed, 'Naughty boy,' even though every inch of my body tingled with desire."

"Of course," Starr mimicked grinning like a Cheshire cat.

"At any rate, after a few more sensuous innuendos, I caved under his sweet nothings and decided to reveal the necklace."

Starr shook her head, laughing. "Why, you royal tart!"

We both enjoyed a hearty laugh. I cleared my throat to capture her attention again.

"At any rate, I scampered off to my boudoir excited to disrobe. I chose to put on my sheerest skin colored nightshirt with small brass buttons down the front that are so easy to pop open. I freshened up gently rubbing my favorite lilac dusting powder on as much of my body as I could reach. Of course, romancing him was on my mind, but not wanting to appear too eager, I covered my lack of clothing as if out of modesty with my favorite Chinese red silk dressing gown."

The gypsy, not surprised by my decision, quipped, "Modest, huh? I'll bet you were just as anxious to show off that plump bosom of yours as the necklace."

I winked, eager to continue. "I returned to the sitting room and sat down next to him. He was quite the gentleman."

"'Madam, you smell so fresh and lovely as if you just came in from the garden.'" He looked at the sash holding my dressing gown closed. "'Please allow me to open your dressing gown just a bit to take a peek at that wonderful necklace.'"

Of course, I was delighted to oblige. I stood and removed my hand

31

holding my robe closed. As I dropped it to the floor, I watched with anticipation as his blue eyes grew enormous, darting from my naked bosom under my sheer nightshirt to my necklace. He was speechless. I do have that effect on men, you know. Anyway, he mumbled something about extreme beauty. I believed he was noting my physique, but in actuality, it was the gold and gems he was talking about. Silly boy. I forgave him, popping open my nightshirt and allowing his eyes to feast on my voluptuous body, but as he did, his speech became more conniving."

"'My lady, as magnificent as your necklace is, it pales in comparison to your beautiful body. I am humbled to view both.'"

"He stood and pulled me in close to him wanting to feel every part of me. He stopped, kissed me, and deepened the kiss. I was mesmerized by his romantic innuendos."

"'Shall we toast to our afternoon of delightful romance with a glass of sipping sherry?' he said."

"I should have refused, but I repeat lust overtook common sense. At my age, how could I say no? I was accustomed to romancing stable hands and traveling knights, none near as polite or fresh smelling. Anyway, he had already poured the sherry into two glasses while I was disrobing. He handed me my glass before lifting his."

"'Here's to your necklace and an afternoon of lustful pleasures.'"

"With that, we drank sherry until the decanter was half empty. Then, in a moment of weakness, he repeated his hope."

"'I am a jeweler who specializes in fine antique reproductions. If I could make just one woman as sexual as you by just wearing a copy of that necklace, think of how happy she would be.'"

"Before I could answer, he kissed me again."

"'You realize that if I sell the copies in the future, I'd have to return for more instruction. Not just in jewelry design, but in more afternoon delights.'"

"At first, I fought off his idea, shaking my head no, but he was very persistent and his constant gentle touch pleased my senses."

"'My lady, we should share the exquisiteness of your necklace with others from another time as well as share each other's lust. It's like sharing history.'"

He leaned in and kissed the tip of my nose. "'But for today, however, I hope you will share your divine body with mine. Please, my darling, remove your clothes entirely. Allow me the privilege of admiring the necklace against your naked body.'"

"Such a handsome silver tongued young lad speaking to a lonely woman of my age, again, how could I refuse? Hoping to seduce him, I agreed, stood, and dropped my open nightshirt to the floor. I bared my body to him and was eager to do so anticipating the most romantic tryst of my dreams, but alas, his eyes still spent more time on my jewelry than me."

"I realized I had to seduce him further. Moving closer to him, I sat down naked on his lap. He kissed my midriff as his stare soaked in my entire body. My bold movements were working. I lay down resting my head on a pillow as his muscular hands held onto my waist. I felt free to share my deepest desires with him. He caressed and kissed every part of me, his touch mesmerizing while his kisses warmed my body like the sun. This handsome stranger took my mind and body hostage with his passion."

"He moved his wet kisses up to my breasts, then slowly up my neck before meeting my waiting lips."

"As he deepened the kiss, my mind and body became lost in the most sensuous haze. I felt like I would pass out in a sexual fog."

"Oh Starr, I should have known better, but he seemed too good to be true. I just couldn't resist the man's advances. At that moment, my body quivered with such a deep desire like I have never felt before. I wanted him to make love to me right then and there."

I paused to catch my breath before continuing.

"We royals do get lonely, you know. As I drank some more sherry, my lips trembled, eager to meet his again, while my mind became more and more foggy."

I glanced over at Starr just as her sun bronzed skin flushed with color. She reached for my lavender lace fan, opened it, and started to fan herself.

Chapter Three

"My, my, Amelia, you are giving me hot flashes."

I smiled. "Should I stop?"

"No, no, by all means, please continue."

"Minton caressed me as he whispered that I was his dream lover, and he'd like to carry me to my boudoir and show me his true passion. Oh Starr, at that moment, I thought I had died and gone to heaven! How could an older woman such as I decline such a romantic offer?"

Starr quipped, "I'm sure it would be difficult, especially with your past, my dear."

Ignoring her last remark, I kept up with my story. "Quite right. At any rate, we stood and I picked up my nightshirt before he lifted me in his strong young arms and carried me to my bed. I remember how hazy my mind was. At the time, I attributed that to the heat of passion. We made love in the middle of the day over and over again until we both fell asleep. Young men have such bullish stamina, but I'm sure all of this must sound so romantic to a woman of your age. You are older in regular time years than I?"

Starr, still fanning herself, was not happy with my last remark. I realized those words were inappropriate considering I was the one who needed her help.

She looked irritated. "How kind of you to mention, dear. Go on."

"I awoke later that afternoon to pistol shots, only to find the scoundrel gone. I felt my barren neck and searched my nightstand only to discover that my necklace, my inheritance, was gone as well. My maid came to inform me that Minton had killed my most trusted guard, Arthur. My nightshirt open, my head swirling, I realized he must have slipped something into my glass when I went to change. Trust me that was the only way he could remove my necklace from my body. At that point, I knew I had to call on you for help. Starr, I am at a tremendous loss. What am I to do?"

The gypsy looked at me, concerned. "We will work our magic. I will help find your necklace. Don't fret, but I will need to know more of your story," she answered.

I nodded. "My staff was in tears. A guardsman had been murdered, shot in the heart trying to prevent that sham of a Traveler from evaporating into thin air. I felt as if my own heart had been pierced as deeply as my guard's. That imposter came to me with the sole intent of stealing my necklace to sell it at future prices. How stupid of me! How could I even think that someone as young and handsome as he could be interested in a thirty-two year old woman?"

Starr's kind eyes said it all as she touched my hand. "Don't worry my friend, we'll track that scoundrel down. Don't beat yourself up. You are very beautiful. By today's dating standards, you're a very desirable woman."

I puzzled at her last remark. "Really? Well, maybe I should transplant myself here and look for someone I met on my last visit. Oh, I almost forgot your rules of Travel. That horrible seven-day rule. If I remain any longer than that, I become my accurate age, which as you so kindly stated on my last visit, was dust. Enough daydreaming. Anyway, I have a drawing of the necklace. Give me a moment. Oh yes, here it is. I knew I placed it on the table."

I took great care to straighten the folds in the paper before handing the drawing to Starr. She studied the pencil sketch of me sporting a low-cut dress and wearing my necklace with pride. The artist had only colored in the iris of my eyes along with the green of the emeralds, the

36

yellow diamonds, along with the white and yellow gold chain. He said his rendering would be more dramatic that way.

"What a magnificent piece of jewelry," Starr studied the drawing, noting its intricate detail of my necklace. "This is an heirloom fit for a queen."

"Yes, my sister," I responded without hesitation. "'Tis indeed. 'Tis proof that I am in line for the throne of England, be it fourth removed."

Starr smiled. "That's closer than I'll ever get. Now tell me more about the Traveler. Did he happen to say where he was from?"

I leaned back in my chair and took a deep breath. My mind reviewed every conversation with him, such as they were. At last, I remembered something. My face flushed like a torch.

"Why yes, he did when he first asked about meeting the craftsmen. He didn't look Spanish, but he said something about Floreeda. You know, the New World."

"Florida. You do remember that I live in Ft. Myers, Florida?"

"Now I do. I only remembered Washington, D.C. but that is where you sent me to find Duke."

"Yes, that's right. Amelia, tell me, did he mention a location in Florida?"

Starr leaned forward. I sensed the gypsy was testing me. I thought carefully.

"Oh, I do remember! He said that he was from a peculiar sounding place called Meamie."

"Miami?"

"Yes, yes, that's it, Miami. He worked at a market of jewelry. It sounded like a gentleman's name … Seymour?"

"Seymour … Seymour … Seybold?" Starr asked. I sensed she was trying as hard as she could to narrow down the location.

"Starr, you truly have the gift. That was the name he gave me.

37

Seybold."

"You said his name was Minton."

"Why, yes, Starr. Do you honestly think I could be so intimate with a man whose name I did not know?"

The gypsy grinned, refusing to answer that question. Looking like she already knew the answer, she continued to persevere with questions, much like the King's Guard.

"Let's hope he gave you his real name. Did he know that you have a gypsy seer to aid in your Time Travel?"

"Of course not. Only Alden knows of our arrangement. He has been sworn to secrecy. I confide in no one, not even my most trusted servant. That's our secret."

Starr looked pleased by my discretion.

"Good, Amelia. He may have given you his real name, then."

As Starr finished that thought, she looked up at the clock on her wall. "Oh dear, it's almost time for my next appointment. I became so wrapped up in your story I almost forgot. Please go upstairs and freshen up. Enjoy a bath and a shampoo. You know where everything is. Help yourself to whatever you would like to wear in my closet. Try to choose some lighter clothes. Time Travel in velvet clothing to eighty plus degree heat can make for pungent body odor. No offense intended."

"None taken, but I bathed last Sunday."

"I don't care. Go do as I say. Don't come down until you do. Please wait until I call you. When I do, go by the name of Amy. I pride myself in keeping my appointments as confidential as possible, so you won't hear from me until after this gentleman has left."

I nodded, but when she mentioned "gentleman," she piqued my curiosity. What are all these lonesome men like? Of course, I couldn't ask so I scampered upstairs and rushed through my bath and shampoo. I remembered during my last visit, at being amazed how the water just flowed from a pipe into the tub.

Drying my hair with a towel, I rummaged through her closet, selecting the most flattering outfit I could find, a turquoise peasant style dress. Funny style, it had a very high neckline with a skirt above the ankles. Even though this was my second visit, the styles of this time still felt odd to a lady of my standing. I found an emerald green floral sash and tied it around my waist. Brushing my wet hair, I remembered I had one more item to stash. I sat on the bed in my room and removed a velvet bag from my travel skirt. I tiptoed around Starr's guest quarters looking for a good hiding place. I then hid my bag in the very back of the top nightstand drawer. I covered it with small towels before dressing and combing my hair.

Just in time, I heard the bell on the gypsy's front door ring. Curious, I raced to the top of the landing. I watched as Starr opened the front door. I soon heard a male voice speak first.

"Good morning. Ma'am. Are you Starr Knight?"

What? Could it be? I know that voice! Soft, masculine, with just the right amount of shyness. My heart danced to the sound of each delightful syllable. Definitely familiar. One I have dreamed of hearing every day since my last visit! Could it really be him? If only I had a better view. I leaned over the railing as far as I could without tumbling. *Do my eyes deceive me? It is him. It's really him! It's Ryan.*

Ryan Redstone. My joyful mind drifted back to our meeting when I searched for my Duke in the place they kept abandoned dogs. I was heartbroken after I found Duke's shelter cage empty. Desperate, my eyes scanned the adoption room looking for my dog until I saw him in the arms of this delightful man.

He looked at me and whispered as if not knowing what to say. "Um, it's nice to meet another animal lover." Ryan then looked down at his shoes before blurting out, "Maybe I could buy you a cup of coffee and Duke some water in the shelter coffee shop to celebrate your reunion after you finish your paperwork?"

My heart raced like a hound chasing a fox. My mind worked overtime. *Why is this happening now? Why couldn't I meet a man like*

39

him in my own time? I must smile and not discourage him. I have to remain discreet to get Duke home safely.

"I'm afraid I cannot right now. I'm in a bit of a hurry."

"Maybe some other time, then."

I could tell it was difficult for him to ask me to join him. I couldn't understand why. He was so handsome.

Ryan then reached in his top pocket and handed me a card with his name on it. "This is where I work. I understand your hesitation. It's difficult these days to trust a perfect stranger."

He then held his hand out to shake. I returned the gesture but my hand went limp in his. The mere touch of his hand made me tingle. He was so delightful I wanted to take him home and romance him at once. His gentle touch was so unlike the rowdy lovers I took to bed at my manor. He held my hand for a while as we stared into each other's eyes again. His gaze melted into mine as those sparks intensified into desire.

"Please. You are so very beautiful. What is your name?"

"Amelia. My name is Amelia."

"Amelia, that's a lovely name. I don't hear it often, but by coincidence, I'm researching someone by that name and found its origin to mean "beloved" and "industrious." Not a bad combination. I sense that description may suit you to a T. Perhaps we'll meet again."

"Perhaps," I answered with a hint of remorse realizing I thought that could never happen. Oh, how I wished it could! And now it finally did!

My heart pounded so hard at the thought of seeing him again, I thought I might lose my balance. Straightening, I decided to listen, anxious to hear about this gorgeous man who held my heart in the palm of his hand. He appeared as reluctant and shy as he did that day in the shelter. Starr motioned for him to enter.

"You must be Mr. Redstone. Please come in."

"Thank you. I am Ryan Redstone."

Ryan Redstone. Just those words were music to my ears. I couldn't believe the fortunate coincidence. Starr instructed him to follow her into her reading room. Ryan appeared cautious as he followed the gypsy, taking in the ambiance of his surroundings.

I remembered the words on Starr's sign: FINDER OF TRUE LOVE. From the looks of all the photos of happy couples on her wall, I was sure she was well qualified for such a task. But I still puzzled about why such a handsome man would need the services of a matchmaker. I wanted to learn more about the man I couldn't get out of my mind.

As quiet as a church mouse, I moved down the stairway and stooped in the shadows so I could peek into the reading room. I'm sure Starr thought I was primping, so she left the reading room door open a crack. How fortunate for me. I could see and hear everything.

Ryan held the chair for Starr. No surprise. He struck me as a proper gentleman. He sat down next to her at the table. From where I sat, I could watch his every expression. Ryan appeared nervous, squirming in his seat while adjusting his monocles every few minutes. The gypsy commenced the conversation.

"Mr. Redstone, as you know, my name is Starr Knight. My prowess as a finder of true love is well-known in many worlds and different times. My success can be easily documented. I will be happy to tell you anything you need to know about what I do and how we will begin our search."

Ryan, looking up at all the photos of happy couples, answered, "Please call me Ryan. Don't take offense at what I'm about to say. I'm not sure I'm ready for this. I'm still uncomfortable with the thought of seeing a matchmaker, let alone baring my soul to a total stranger. Some of my friends thought it might help me feel alive again, but I'm just not sure. Rest assured whatever direction I take, I'll pay you for your time."

Starr acknowledged his concern with a caring smile.

"Ryan, I take great pride in what I do. My skills have been passed down to me from my grandmother. Your happiness is far more important to me than money. Just look at all the photos of happy couples I've

41

helped. My clients' welfare and discretion are always my utmost concern."

I watched Starr touch the top of his hand. He did not take it away, listening to her every word as she continued.

"I'm here for you when you're ready. No hurry … no stress. If you want to do this another time or not at all, I respect your decision."

Ryan squeezed Starr's hand.

"You have a special kindness about you. You remind me of my Aunt Judy. As kids, we could tell her anything and knew our childhood secrets were safe. I wish I knew what to do now. On one hand, I want to tell you, but on the other, I have never spilled my feelings to a total stranger."

Starr paused. "If you'd feel better, take a few days to think about it. You have my number. If you decide to proceed, we'll make another appointment."

Ryan shrugged.

"I came such a long way to do this … to meet with you and I hope to find true love again. I'm leaving at the end of the week to stay in Miami for a work project."

Ryan put his head in his hands. I could sense Starr wanted to calm him down.

"Perhaps a cup of tea will help you relax. I'll be right back."

When Starr left the room, I moved back into the shadows of the stairway. She returned with a tray carrying a pot of tea and some sugar cookies shaped like stars.

"I made them myself. Please try one."

Ryan reached in and took a cookie as Starr poured two cups of tea.

"I don't believe this. Aunt Judy made sugar cookies that tasted just like these. Of course, hers were round. Are you psychic as well?"

"Let's just say I love making people happy."

"Well, you sure surprised me. I think we can start but not with the most personal things. That is, if it's acceptable to you."

"That's fine. Now, whenever you feel uncomfortable, just stop. I understand. Why don't we begin with likes and dislikes, favorite things to do, favorite movies, maybe special interests? Would that be all right?"

Ryan, still munching on Starr's cookies, nodded his head as he responded.

"Yes, I can do that."

Starr glanced up when she heard a sudden noise. *Oh, those dreadful creaky floorboards!* She got up and pushed on the door. Luckily, it didn't close all the way. I tiptoed down the stairs and hid to the right of the crack in the door. I heard Starr again.

"Tell me, what do you like to do for fun?"

Ryan smiled as he told her about Stormy, the black Labrador retriever he adopted a couple of years ago. He talked happily about their walks in the park and playing ball. Starr interrupted.

"Do you have a picture of Stormy?"

Ryan reached in his pocket and handed Starr a small piece of paper. She held it for a few minutes, looking pleased at what she saw.

"I can sense you two are a perfect match. How did you find him?"

"I adopted him or should I say he adopted me from a shelter."

Starr smiled. "Smart dog. May I borrow this? It will help my search. I will return it as soon as we find the right woman."

Ryan agreed before telling her about something called movies. I heard him say,

"My favorite is 'Somewhere in Time.' It is very romantic. Have you seen it?"

Starr shook her head.

"It tells the story of two lovers from different times. She is from the past, he from the present."

Be still my heart; there may be hope for me yet. He went on to discuss his favorite books and plays and before moving on to his work.

"I love my job. I enjoy reading about history and doing the research necessary to complete any transaction. I am very lucky. Most people go to work because they have to. I have to work but I love what I do."

Starr seized on that moment.

"That's wonderful, Ryan. Please, when you're ready, tell me more about you."

After a few minutes of silence, Ryan spoke.

"I feel like I've lost my purpose in life, my compass to navigate through my daily stress. I do love my work and absorb myself in it to bury my deep feelings of loneliness and sadness. Five years ago, the love of my life, Jillian, died one day before we were to celebrate our tenth anniversary. She's always in my heart and on my mind. I think about her daily. Everything I do; every place I go reminds me of us. Stormy, my rescue dog, has been my only redemption. He brings a joy and unconditional love to my life. I want to get up every morning and take him for his walk. I know I need to feel that same kind of companionship and love from a woman. Stormy and I believe we're both ready for that next step now. I guess all you have to do is find a woman willing to accept both of us."

He placed his head in his hands.

"I have been at loss with no idea how to find companionship again. I'm not into the bar scene and anytime a friend introduces me to someone, she does not hold a candle to my Jillian. As I already wrote to you, I work long hours as an appraiser and acquirer at the Smithsonian in Washington, D.C. in the antique jewelry department. I don't meet many people socially except for our donors and sellers because I must study and travel a great deal for each acquisition."

I held my breath. I still couldn't believe he was here, and not in Washington, D.C. where I found Duke!

I pulled myself together to listen further.

"How did you hear of me?" Starr asked, looking sympathetic.

"Someone at the museum asked if I ever considered consulting a professional matchmaker. The rest of the group at lunch that day just laughed at the thought. I did too, even though I felt the suggestion worth pursuing. I couldn't bear the thought of talking to a matchmaker at home. One of my co-workers was sure to find out. When I learned that work related issues would bring me to Florida, I searched online for such services. I planned this side trip to visit the Ft. Myers—Sanibel area as a mini working vacation and hoped to make an appointment to coincide with that. I started looking for someone like yourself who might not be too far away from where I planned to stay. After I read about you online, I sent you an e-mail, ready to make an appointment. I do hope you are as discreet as your past clients say you are in their recommendations."

I listened as their conversation answered some of my questions … the most important being he was not spoken for. I watched Starr reach for his hand again and look straight into his eyes.

"My goal is to make you happy in love. Our visit will remain confidential."

I heard Ryan take a deep breath and watched as he relaxed his shoulders.

"I'm relieved to hear that. I see by all the photos you have brought happiness to many couples. One more question, if I may. When I read in an article in an online paranormal journal about you, it said that you work with Time Travelers. Is that for real?"

Starr sat back. I could sense by her expression that she was uncomfortable with his question. She twisted around in her seat, pointing to a wedding photo of a happy couple on the sideboard behind her. "Ryan, please look at that joyful couple. Olivia came to me distraught after her groom abandoned her at the altar. She didn't know how to cope with what happened until I introduced her to Devlin, a shy but loving accountant from the small town next to hers. It was love at first sight. You do know, I can make this happen for you too if you let me."

45

I was sure it was in an effort to distract him. It did not work because he repeated his question.

Once more, he asked, "Starr, I'm curious. Do you work with Travelers?"

After a brief hesitation, she responded.

"Yes, I do. Tell me, do you believe Time Travel can happen?"

"I can't say for sure. I have some scientist friends who do and are trying to make it happen. I won't rule it out. Anyway, that's not why I'm here. That's just an inquisitive side note."

"You must know by now that I'm a serious guy, on the reserved side, not what you call impetuous. It'll take a special woman to be interested in me. I don't like crowds and enjoy studying history. I am looking for a sweet woman, preferably near my age. I just turned thirty-six. She should have a little spunk to make up for what I lack."

I listened with great interest as my handsome Ryan finished pouring his heart out to Starr. *How fortunate! Ryan's description of the woman he'd like to meet sounded just like me.* I considered staying there a little longer to take advantage of my position, peeking in and out to get a better look.

I did. Just as I remembered, he was built quite solid with a kind face and gentle eyes. Starr focused like a laser on her client, unaware I was staring at Ryan through the crack in the doorway.

"How long will you be in Florida?"

"I assume my work will keep me in the state about one month, but I'll only be a couple of hours away in Miami. While I'm there, if you find the right person, I can travel back and forth."

The gypsy stared deep into Ryan's eyes.

"Good. I'll have plenty of time to plant the seeds of romance. I always tell my clients that romance is better by chance than by arrangement. Trust me. We shall meet again tomorrow at this time. I will have some photos for you to look at, along with bios. After you select one, a meeting will just happen."

Ryan sounded surprised.

"So soon? That's great news. I am ready to start anew."

Starr set out at once to work her magic. She placed her rose-colored crystal ball in front of her. From the hallway, I could see a kaleidoscope of different shades of pink and blue circle the walls.

"Ryan, as I gaze into my crystal ball, I can see many prospects for you. I see happiness in your future with a woman you will feel passionate about. I'll compose a list for you to peruse. Shall we meet again tomorrow afternoon, say at two?"

By now I was fuming! *Ha! One of these women had better be me.* I waited, anxious to hear if Ryan would return tomorrow.

"Tomorrow will be fine. I'm feeling better already."

I watched as Ryan got up to leave. He reached into his pocket, I thought for money, but stopped when he spotted a piece of wrinkled paper on the other end of the table.

Oh no! How could that careless woman leave my drawing on the table? It was meant for her eyes only. I watched with trepidation as Ryan picked up the drawing to get a closer look. Will he recognize me? Will he say something to Starr? When we first met, I didn't want him to know who I really was.

Ryan adjusted his monocles. "Well, what's this? The paper looks old, like it might be an old sketch or document. Mind if I have a look?"

By now I was so mad smoke could form steam in my ears. How careless. And to think she was the one I trusted to help me. I saw Starr was caught off guard by her own negligence. Ryan was careful holding onto the corners of my document with his fingertips. At that point, she had no choice but to let him look. *And she thinks I'm the cheeky tart.*

Starr hesitated for a moment before speaking.

"Why no, Ryan. Please have a look, but be careful I would like to keep it in good condition. It's not mine but belongs to someone I'm

47

helping."

I watched with baited breath as he examined what I held most dear. He placed the parchment back down on the table examining it with the utmost care. As he scrutinized the paper, I could see his eyes said it all.

"This is a magnificent sketch from the eighteenth century of a royal lady. Do you know who she is? Odd, I have this strong feeling I've seen her likeness before. Who is she?"

Starr remained quiet as Ryan continued. "How did you acquire this? It looks original and could be very valuable."

By now, the gypsy fumbled for words. "As I stated earlier, a friend gave it to me recently for helping her."

"Do you have any idea who's pictured in this drawing?"

Starr remained calm. She obviously did not want to reveal her hand. Ryan pushed anxious to learn more.

"Please tell me ... tell me everything you know about this woman."

He looked back at Starr. "This is what I do for work. I know about the necklace she is wearing. It is famous in English history known as the Abbington crown jewels. This is an historic piece of jewelry designated by a king to represent the entitlement of duchy to its designated rather than rightful heir. As you can see, it's large and heavy, in a yellow and white gold chain with gemstones. This chain of royal lineage can be worn by a gentleman or a lady. It's very odd that you received this recently. I'll ask again, are you psychic?"

Starr looked at Ryan careful of her answer. "I've been told by others I have the gift."

He examined my drawing further. "Is your client a man or woman?"

"Why do you ask?"

Ryan paused. He rubbed his forehead, seeming to be a bit taken back by the situation.

"I ask because The Abbington Necklace is what brought me to

Florida. A jeweler who works out of the Seybold building in Miami claims to be in possession of the original and wants to sell it to The Smithsonian. One never knows. So many scam artists are out there hoping for that quick buck. Any rate, that's why the museum sent me here to authenticate the acquisition before any investment is made on behalf of the Board of Directors."

Starr perked up like she'd found buried treasure. "The owner of the sketch is a woman."

Ryan looked at the drawing again. "If she looks anything like the woman in this sketch, she must be very beautiful."

After that statement, I knew I was ready to make my entrance, but Starr blurted out another question before I could do so. "Are you to hear from this man soon?"

"Why yes. He's to contact me sometime in the next few days, as a matter of fact, to set up a meeting."

I clung to his every word but couldn't believe my ears. I fumed and rejoiced at the same time. First, I find Ryan! Ryan, the man of my dreams, was also my path to finding the greedy scalawag who stole my jewels and killed Arthur! Now I had to plot how to get Ryan's heart while piercing Minton's. It was a difficult task, even for a woman with my superior skills.

I listened as Ryan continued.

"We have a donor ready to purchase the necklace for two million dollars and place it in the museum. I came, not only to authenticate the piece, but also to take care of business. As a matter of fact, I hope to examine that very necklace in a few days."

Chapter Four

Ugh! A few days had better be less than seven. With that last remark, I could no longer control myself. I burst into the room like a bolt of summer lightning. Ryan stepped back, startled by my entrance. Starr glared at me with such intensity I could feel her anger. I flashed my most winning smile at Ryan, batting my eyelashes.

"Please, do excuse me, Starr. I see you have a guest. It was difficult for me to see from upstairs."

My stare intensified as my eyes met Ryan's. My gaze lingered on his muscular build and gentle face. Ryan smiled. Lucky for me, he was left speechless by my entrance. I winked. When Starr turned to put her crystal ball back, I placed my fingers over my lips to signal to Ryan that we should keep our past meeting a secret. He nodded as I flirted.

"My, my, you handsome man, you could make any lady blush."

His face flushed with color. I could tell he didn't know how to respond to such a bold comment. I was not ashamed. After all, if I liked something, I spoke up and I liked him.

Ryan studied my face. I was not being vain. I had been around enough men to sense he thought me a beauty. It took a few moments before Ryan answered my audacious comment. He cleared his throat.

"Yes, of course, we should be properly introduced. My name is Ryan Redstone. I am in Florida for work and vacation, and you are …?"

Starr was not happy about this so I responded with alacrity. She scowled at our introduction.

"I am Amy Abbington from England."

"Abbington? Has anyone ever told you that you bear an uncanny resemblance to the woman in this drawing?"

He pointed to the sketch on the table.

I blushed in my made-up way men love.

"Why I do believe I have heard that before. I am related to many dukes and duchesses. You know, I'm sure family traits were passed down among all of us. I take it you've heard of my family lineage in Abbington? It is not one of the more famous ones but does go back quite a long way."

Ryan's eyes lingered on mine.

"Yes, I have. As a matter of fact, I'm researching part of your family lineage for The Smithsonian now. This is quite a wonderful coincidence, in more ways than one."

If looks could kill, Starr would have flung an arrow through my heart with her eyes.

"Amy, weren't you freshening up upstairs? Why don't you go back and finish?"

I ignored her comment, keeping my eyes glued on that handsome man.

"I've finished. I feel so much better now. Thank you. I need a break from Travel. Maybe I could help Mr. Redstone fill in some of the blanks about the Abbington heirs. We English do love our history, you know."

Ryan agreed very quickly.

"I'm sure you do. I think I am interested in your personal one, as well. Please tell me all you can about both."

That was all I needed to hear. Not wasting one second, I put his arm in mine.

"Why don't we go out back to Starr's patio where it's a bit more private? Shall we?"

Starr tried to stop us. She always kept a watchful eye on her Travelers and sensed I was up to no good.

"Amy, please. Ryan has no time for that."

He gazed into my eyes.

"I think I could make time for this lovely lady."

Got him! I escorted him out of the room. We walked to Starr's patio consisting of varied colored stone. A peaceful place, it was surrounded by a beautiful garden. I chatted all the way about how the colorful flowers reminded me of my gardens at home. Leading him to a white wicker bench under a white trellis loaded with mauve roses in full bloom, I sat down and reached for his hand. He had a firm grip. I squeezed his hand and pulled him down on the bench next to me.

"Ryan. You are unforgettable. I have thought of no one else since our meeting."

He nodded.

"I've thought of you too. I never saw you again, not in the park or town. I even went back to the shelter hoping I might run into you again, but I had no such luck."

I blurted out. "That would have been impossible."

Ryan looked puzzled by that remark so I tried to diminish its importance.

"I'll tell you why another time. For now, tell me about yourself. I'm sure my story will seem a bit boring in comparison."

Ryan let go of my hand. I desired him to hold me so I lifted his arm and placed it around my waist. He attempted to take it back, but I was too quick for that. I grabbed his hand, again returning it to my waist. Uncomfortable, he slid away from me on the bench and turned, trying as hard as he could not to look at me, but I was determined to break through his shyness. Moving closer, I shook my head, letting my long curls softly touch his face. I stood up directly in front of him, took both his hands, and placed them on my waist once more. He didn't fight this time. His eyes took in the curves of my body.

"Amy ... may I call you that? You are a beautiful, intelligent woman. I'm afraid I'm the one who's a bore. I study all the time, history with a specialty in antique jewelry. I work for The Smithsonian Museum in Washington, D.C."

I sat back down pursing my lips.

"Washington, D.C.? That's where my Duke was taken."

"Taken? I thought he was lost."

"No, he was taken. Where exactly is Washington, D.C.?"

Ryan laughed. "You're pulling my leg, aren't you?"

"Don't think I'm that strong."

Ryan answered with a smile. "That's our capital city. It's a little over one thousand miles north of here."

"Oh, I knew I had been somewhere in the New World."

He laughed some more. I was glad my answers amused him. Humor might be the best way to penetrate his shyness.

"Besides being lovely, you do have quite the sense of humor."

"I am English and we Brits are noted for our humor. I'm not current on all of your customs, so they may need a bit of explaining. Let me tell you about me. I live in a beautiful manor house that once belonged to the Duke of Abbington. I am his direct descendant. I am thirty-two years of age and still unmarried, much to the dismay of my relatives. Starr is a very dear old friend. I need her help to settle a family dispute."

"The Abbington Manor? Huh? I thought a duke lived there now. I'm working on a research problem regarding the sudden appearance of his family jewels."

I nodded.

"Yes, as I understand, those jewels have been missing for a long time. Quite a travesty for the lineage, you know."

He looked at me quite serious.

"I can only imagine. You said you were single. I am too. I was married for ten years to the most wonderful woman. I lost my wife five years ago, in an accident. I miss her dearly. She was always a great help to me in matters of life and work. When you've had your heart broken this way, it's difficult to imagine finding love again. That's why I was searching for a dog at the shelter that day. When I learned Duke was yours, I adopted a dog, Stormy, a week later to try and fill that nagging hole in my heart. Tell me, Amy, have you ever been in love?"

"No, Ryan. Sadly, no. Many men have courted me, but none attracted my eye until I met you. Do you think me fussy?"

"No. Smart. Cautious. It's hard to turn your heart over to someone. When that love comes to an end, it shatters your very existence."

As I brushed some strands of hair away from his eyes. I could see them tearing up. I removed my lace handkerchief from my bodice and wiped them.

"Sounds to me like you were fortunate enough to have had that kind of love."

"Yes, I was one of the lucky ones. I had the most wonderful wife. Wonderful. His eyes teared as he spoke. Jillian and I had been married for almost ten years. She was everything to me, my soul mate, my life partner. On the eve of our tenth anniversary, Jillian was going to work when a drunk driver drove through a stop sign and side-swiped her car thrusting her against the windshield. She had her seatbelt on but died from massive head injuries. When I lost her, I lost everything that mattered in my life. I wanted my own life to end and thought about suicide so she and I could be together again. When we met at the animal shelter, I was looking for a companion and found one when I adopted Stormy."

I saw tears form in the corners of his eyes again. Ryan leaned forward covering his eyes with his hands. I placed both his hands in mine, removing them from his face and held them.

"There, there now, my sweet man. You will find love again. Starr is quite good at that."

I wiped away his tears, leaning over to kiss his cheek. He moved back, surprised at my boldness. I wanted to assure him.

"I hope you do find love again. You are a kind, sensitive man. In the meantime, I would be delighted to help in any way I can with your work project."

As I spoke, he appeared more comfortable. I sat down and moved closer, kissing his cheek again. This time he didn't resist, but rested his head against mine.

"Amy, I have been unbearably lonely. I tried to absorb myself in work, but it doesn't fill the void. I'm at a loss."

I felt his anguish.

"Starr always says love happens when least expected. I'm sure love will happen again for you."

I stared into his clear blue eyes. His soulful gaze swept me away into another world. Such a delightful feeling! I never felt anything like it before. As I turned toward him, I felt the heat of his body against my side. I couldn't help myself. I kissed his cheek, moving my kisses to his lips. He closed his eyes as my lips kissed his. I had waited years for this, and it was worth every minute. I held his hand, lifting it to my face. His touch was soft, gentle, and so different from any of my past lovers. We held our kiss for a while. I released his lips; his eyes softened as he gazed into mine.

"You amaze me, Amy. There is something very special about you. I felt the same way the first time we met. I haven't felt like that since Jillian."

He lifted my hand to his lips and kissed it. My body trembled from the sensitivity of his touch and the softness of his kiss. He took my breath away, but thoughts of my necklace suddenly made me focus again.

"Ryan, I'd love to spend more time with you. Maybe I could share my knowledge of family history and the Abbington jewels. Of course, you must understand that whatever information I have has been passed down by word of mouth from one heir to another. I'm not sure if it will help."

His eyes lit up like Christmas candles.

"Yes, yes, that would help. I appreciate your interest in my work. Since I haven't been able to get you out of my mind for three years, I want to spend more time with you. I take it you don't want Starr to know about our past meeting, so here is not a good place. Maybe we could get together before the intended seller calls me? I've spent hours digging through facts and have a notebook full of research. I have to make sure that his Abbington jewels are genuine and acquired through proper means. Would you meet me for coffee tomorrow morning? It would have to be early, like eight-thirty at The Egg House right around the corner from here. It's a handy spot just across the street from the county library. That's how I found it."

Such relief. I thought he'd never ask to see me again. I was not a morning person but could be for Ryan.

"Eight-thirty in the morning at The Egg House it is. Now, it's such a lovely summer day. Would you care for some chilled tea?"

Ryan laughed. "You are silly. It's warm and May. You mean iced tea?"

"Right," I said as he pulled me up from the wicker bench. I walked him to a patio table and chairs near the back door.

"Now, my handsome man, you wait here while I go fetch the tea."

I quickly scampered into the kitchen and took a pitcher of chilled tea from the ice box, along with two tall glasses from the cupboard. Starr stood in the doorway, blocking my way out. Her back against the door, she yelled out to him.

"Ryan, it's time for you to leave. I have another appointment. I have your cell number. I'll see you tomorrow afternoon at two?"

Starr held me back. I struggled to get through with my tray but stopped for fear I would drop it. Starr appeared adamant.

Ryan answered, sounding a bit surprised. "But Amy just left to bring us iced tea."

Starr refused to listen.

"I'll see you at two tomorrow afternoon, Ryan. Please, it's best if you leave now."

Ryan looked puzzled by Starr's manner, but being a gentleman, he did not argue. "Two tomorrow afternoon. That'll be fine. See you then. Thank you."

Starr glared at me.

"And just what do you think you're going to do to that nice man?"

I had to convince her that, even though I wanted my necklace back, I wouldn't hurt Ryan.

"Trust me. I shan't hurt him. I know what you are thinking. He's the way back to my inheritance. Yes, he may be. But he's as helpless as a lost kitten. I could never hurt a kitten."

With that, I pushed Starr out of the way and went back outside, but by then my prince had already left through the garden gate.

Chapter Five

That next morning, daylight creeping through my window shades woke me from a difficult night's sleep. Still concerned about the fate of my duchy, I had tossed and turned most of the night. I was plagued by the two K's, how to keep Ryan and kill Minton. Ryan was not like any man I'd ever met before. He wanted nothing from me, no bawdy role in the sack … no money for the effort. He wanted only to spend time with me. I worried I would need more than seven days for him to get to know me. Stretching, I raised my arms in the air as high as I could. I yawned, hoping to snap my sleepy mind awake.

All of this time travel can turn a lady's head upside down. I glanced at the small clock on my nightstand. Seven thirty. I needed to rush so as not to be late. I jumped out of bed and dressed in another unfashionable outfit. I added a navy sash to the green skirt and buttoned up the striped navy blue blouse. I hurried the brush through my hair and slapped on some rouge. Ready to meet Ryan at The Egg House, I snuck downstairs past Starr. She was on the phone with a perspective client so she didn't even bother to look up. I tapped the front door closed and tiptoed out without notice.

Anxious to meet Ryan, I wanted to run the two blocks but paced myself into a brisk walk. As I approached the small café, I saw my handsome Ryan sitting outside alone, wearing short brown pants and a light blue linen short sleeved shirt. He looked so crisp, so genteel. I hurried my pace, almost tripping on a crack in the walk. When he looked up, my heart raced as his eyes met mine. I took the fan from my bodice and waved it to cool my blushing face. I was smitten all right, but I had to keep reminding myself of the reason I called on Starr.

You must focus on the necklace, Amelia. Ryan is the frosting on the cake.

The handsome lad waved me over as soon as he spotted me.

I smiled and obliged.

"Amy, please come and sit down. I already ordered a pot of tea, some toast with jam. I hope that's all right."

He stood as I approached.

"That's very kind of you."

I sat down as close to him as I could get. Ryan opened a large leather sack that contained a huge folder of papers. He removed the folder and placed it to the side of his cup. The papers overflowed with all kinds of printed clippings and handwritten notes. He opened the folder to show me its contents.

"This represents my entire research on the Abbington jewels. It's quite extensive if you'd like to browse through it."

Ryan pushed the folder over to me. I opened it. Leafing through some of the articles, I was amazed at all the facts he had accumulated.

"Are these about my jewels, I mean my family's jewels?"

My question took Ryan by surprise. "You said your jewels? Bold, aren't we? Or is that another one of your English jokes? I have to get used to your sense of humor. Yes, this is all about your jewels. Please tell me everything you know about them."

I paused for a few seconds to peruse the articles. My face lit up when I realized what was missing from his research.

"I don't know what I can add to all of this. Just taking a quick look through these, I found no mention of the royal tradesman's mark that identifies the original necklace."

"Yes, you're right. None of these articles show any mention of a mark. What does it look like and where is it?"

I took one of the pictures out of the folder and pointed to where the mark should be.

"The mark, a small crown to indicate royalty, is here on the link next to the claw clasp. It doesn't show on this picture because it is on the other side. If there is no mark, the necklace is a forgery. Oh, how I wish we knew each other just a bit better. I will tell you what I can now but intend to reveal much more later."

The waitress interrupted us. "Your tea, sir". She placed the teapot, two cups and two plates of toast with a jam tray on our table. Ryan picked up the pot and poured the tea.

"Perfect," I remarked, taking a sip of my breakfast tea.

Ryan shot me an inquisitive look. "What do you mean you'll tell me more later? How did you come to know so much about the necklace?"

I gulped my first sip of my tea down. I didn't want to reveal everything just yet, but felt I had to start.

"Okay. It's my turn for a question. Do you believe in Time Travel?"

Ryan took a big bite of his toast. He finished chewing and swallowed hard.

"That's odd. Starr asked me the same thing. I have friends trying to find out if Time Travel is possible. I guess I wouldn't rule it out. Why?"

I took a deep breath, a very deep breath before deciding to answer. "Would it surprise you to learn that I am the Grand Duchess of Abbington?"

Ryan displayed no emotion at my revelation. He suddenly burst into a hearty laugh.

"I thought you said you were single? You mean to tell me you're married to the duke? Why on earth didn't you tell me this yesterday? I found myself attracted to you. I don't want us to start out on the wrong foot. I hoped our relationship would blossom into something romantic as well as one of friendship. I hope this is another one of your English jokes."

I reached for his hand. "Ryan, I *am* single. I'm afraid that my right to the title is twisted. You must trust me on this. I am attracted to you as well. Now, please let me continue."

He sat back, puzzled by my remarks.

"I am Amelia Augusta, Duchess of Abbington, fourth in line to the throne, and direct descendant of the Grand Duke Hestor, who, one hundred years prior, was given the necklace by King Charles to designate his rightful heir. Whoever inherits the necklace inherits the royal title and all rights to the duchy. I am the rightful title holder now."

I saw by Ryan's expression that my admission bewildered him.

"Amy, are you trying to tell me the current resident of Abbington Manor is an imposter? Are you kidding again? That necklace was bestowed to Duke Hestor in 1661. Here, I'll show you. One hundred years later would be 1761. You are either joking or delusional."

I smiled. "Neither, my sweet man." I winked and reached for his hand, looking directly into those gorgeous blue eyes.

"Please trust me. There is an imposter involved, but I promise to explain at the proper time. At any rate, a man came to the manor house claiming to make replicas of antique necklaces. He, I am embarrassed to admit, wined and dined me. In a moment of pure weakness, I showed him the necklace. Alas, I am as lonely as you. Living in a large manor house does not afford me the opportunity to meet many nice men. Anyway, this jeweler claimed he was from Floreeda."

"Florida. You're telling me here."

"Yes, I am. Anyway, he said that he wanted to study my necklace to make his reproductions. I introduced him to our master jewelers before taking him back to the manor. We then ... well, let's just say he caught me off guard, and I trusted him too much. He took the necklace when I was unaware and left."

61

Ryan listened, intent on hearing every word. He looked baffled, not knowing whether or not I was telling the truth, had gone mad or should be committed to an asylum.

"You have to be joking, but for the sake of conversation, I'll play along. The man in question came back to Florida?"

"Yes, I guess you could say that."

"And then what?"

"Well, that's when I contacted Starr for help. She is very good in these situations. She helped me come here."

Ryan sat back in his chair. "You mean she sent you an airline ticket to fly here? That's quite a story. Ever think about writing a book?"

"Guess you could say I flew here. What I'm trying to tell you is the call that I overheard you tell Starr about may lead us, I mean you, to the real necklace."

Ryan stared long and hard at me. He pinched my arm. I squealed.

"You seem real and have your wits about you."

"When we finish here, let's go somewhere private. I'd like to tell you more and show you how I feel about you, if you'd let me."

I was very attracted to him. I felt guilty, hoping to seduce the man I loved into letting me be privy to more information.

Ryan wiggled in his seat. He looked away; I'm sure trying to avoid being taken in by my lingering stare. I knew it made most men desire me, so I would not let up.

"Please. I am for real. Let's go back to where you are staying, and we can talk some more."

I placed my hand on his knee and worked it up his warm leg. Ryan quickly signaled for the waitress.

"Check please."

He turned and looked at me. "I hope you're joking. If not, I may have to have you committed." He laughed a nervous laugh. "Okay, we have a short drive. My hotel is on the river in the downtown area of Ft. Myers."

"Sounds lovely," I answered. "Take me to your carriage."

"Carriage? You're not going to let up on this charade? I'll play along. My lady, our horseless carriage awaits."

We left the Egg House. He walked me to the street and stopped next to a very strange looking silver colored vehicle. I was surprised to see that his carriage was indeed horseless! He opened a side door, and I was eager to jump in. He remained silent during our ride. I saw a large river not too far away. As we approached the river, Ryan turned his carriage into a large building with a sign that read "Riverfront Motel." He spoke to me at last.

"My room's upstairs. Have you visited the river park yet? It's beautiful and just across the street. The river's dark blue waters are edged with lush greens. Loads of birds frequent the park and large and small fish jump near the shoreline. Let's take a quick walk over there before we go upstairs."

How exciting! I had never traveled to the river or coast before. Both were long journeys from my manor. Ryan took my hand and escorted me out of his strange looking carriage. I laughed.

"Your carriage beats my horse and buggy any day!"

Ryan shook his head at my remark. I was sure he thought I was joking.

"Hope so. Come on. It's really nice here."

He led me across the road, through the grass to a long wooden dock built out on the water. Ryan took a deep breath.

"Look at how clear the sky is, how beautiful the water is. I could stay here forever," he told me.

My eyes took in the magnificent scenery, but my gaze always returned to Ryan.

"I, as well," I said, wishing I could remain there with him forever. We walked the path along the river looking at the guesthouses across the way. I spotted a bench and steered him over to it. We sat down, and I pointed to the water.

"Oh, look at the ducks. How happy they are wiggling their little tails in the water. My tail wiggles at the sight of you."

I abruptly pulled him over to me by his shirt collar and kissed him with a long passionate kiss. I held him in my arms as we sat there. I knew I surprised him. He must have enjoyed it because, before I knew it, he leaned in for another. Of course, I was happy to oblige.

"Oh Amy, Amelia Augusta, whatever your name is, I'd like to know a lot more about you. I'm very attracted to you and have been since our first meeting! I want to spend the rest of the day here with you."

I was just as smitten, perhaps a bit more, but struggled to keep my emotions in check. Desperate to get my necklace back, I had to remain focused.

"My dear Ryan, I desire you as well."

We sat there for quite a while, taking in the sights and holding on to each other. That ended all too soon when Ryan looked at his watch.

"It's a quarter past one already. We should head back to Starr's for my appointment."

I didn't want to leave. I could tell I was making progress.

"Why don't you send her a message that you are tied up and will come another time? I'm sure we can find something to do that will allow us to get to know each other better."

I leaned in and kissed him. Ryan moved away from me.

"I would like nothing better but I can't now. I gave her my word. Don't worry I will tell her that I don't want to meet any other women. You and only you are the one that I want. If we tell her about us, we could ask that she give us enough time to get to know each other better."

I couldn't believe my ears. Ryan was a special man and so

honorable. Could my odd feelings be true love? Real love? I remained cautious advising him.

"I think we should keep this our secret until you know who I really am. She will just try to discourage you. Look at her list and thank her. Make another appointment for two days hence. I might have to leave to take care of some pressing business but should return by then."

Ryan helped me up and kissed my hand.

"I'll miss you."

"And I will miss you, as well."

I would miss him, but I realized that I was on day two, and this gentleman was as slow as a land turtle in romance, not to mention information. I had to convince Starr to send me back for two days so I had more time to complete my two K's. We walked back to his carriage, and in no time returned to Starr's. I slipped in the back door while Ryan kept his appointment. I wondered how many beautiful women she was showing him, hoping none would peak his interest. After he left, I waited for the proper time to talk to Starr. She remained in her reading room, going through receipts, when I approached.

"Starr, may I come in? I need to talk to you. It's about the necklace."

"Of course. Come and sit down next to me. What's troubling you?"

"I do not think seven days is long enough to find it. I need more time."

"That's impossible. You know the Travelers' Rule."

"Yes, I do. Quite well, since I have been here before. I wondered if you'd send me back to my manor house for two days. I could check on things at home. You know how I worry about my precious Dukey. I would thereby be extending my time upon my return. Please Starr, please."

She studied my expression.

"Of course, that handsome Mr. Redstone has nothing to do with your decision. He was disinterested in all the photos I showed him. I suspect you had something to do with that."

"I won't lie to you. He is a handsome lad and one of the most

65

genteel men I have ever met, but I must remain focused on the purpose of my visit. In order to locate Minton and retrieve my necklace, I need more time."

"I see. There's no harm in that as long as you promise not to break Mr. Redstone's fragile heart. When were you thinking of Traveling?"

"As soon as possible. Now, if that can be arranged ..."

"I guess now is as good a time as any. You know the risks. You could get caught in a time warp where the winds may not pick you up again."

"I understand, but I'm willing to take that risk. My necklace is my life."

"All right, then. Please stand against the wall over there and face the window."

I did as instructed. Starr waved her arms in the air and looked straight out that window.

"Winds of time. Powerful winds of time. Take Amelia back to her manor house. Come take her now!"

I knew what to expect, but the intense sound of those winds always amazed me. They approached with more speed than I remembered. At first, the winds seeped almost unnoticed under the door until I heard their robust sounds swirl around the reading room. With the might of a small whirlwind, they grabbed me, picking me up in the cyclone and spinning me around through the atmosphere like a child's top. We traveled over the warm waters of the Gulf across land to the open sea. I looked down to see large ships change into smaller sailing vessels with sails blowing in the wind. They never slowed down nor gave warning.

All of a sudden ... crash!

Chapter Six

I landed in my upstairs parlor on the hardwood floor. Madeline was cleaning in the next room when she heard a loud noise and rushed in with Duke barking at her heels. Surprised to find me on the floor, she rushed over to help me up.

"My lady. This is a welcome but unexpected surprise. When did you arrive home? I didn't hear you open the front door. You know how that creaks so. At any rate, I'm so glad you're here. There were some complications soon after you left. While you were away, we had a problem with your cousins, the earls. They kept coming around every other day asking where you and the necklace were. Thaddeus claimed one of your disgruntled stable hands told them he saw a man steal it before disappearing into thin air. This ungrateful servant insists on keeping the rumors alive by telling anyone who will listen that you haven't found it yet. Those two annoying sniveling whiners will do and say anything to covet your duchy."

Madeleine took a lace handkerchief from her apron pocket and wiped some perspiration from her brow. "I felt uneasy and did not know what to say but knew I had to say something hoping to appease their anger. I told them you were visiting an old friend and took your necklace with you as you always do. They vowed to return every day if necessary until they saw you and the necklace together in person."

~ * ~

My mind wandered. Ugh those nasty cousins. They are scoundrels of the lowest kind not deserving of the title of earl. I'm ashamed to call

67

them relatives. They have tried to steal, dupe, and trick me out of my necklace in any way possible. They know my penchant for good looking men and used that against me to steal my necklace.

I remember one day a few years ago, when a very handsome and muscular stableman showed up at my manor inquiring about any odd jobs. He was tanned with bronze eyes and arms like Adonis and said his name was Henry, as if his name even mattered to me. Well, he was such a fine specimen that I had only one odd job on my mind, but first I had to find a way to seduce him. I told him to wait in the foyer for a few minutes and I would escort him to the stable. I dashed into a side room and removed all those horrible layers of petticoats necessary for a lady of my standing as well as any undergarments. Ready, I went back out to the hall and informed him that one of my horses needed new hooves, a fact that was actually true, so I walked with him to the stable and showed him Buttercrust.

Buttercrust, my pride and joy Andulusian golden tan and brown mare, nayed acknowledging my presence so I patted her snout.

I encouraged Henry to do the same before I lured him to a private corner of the stable telling him that was where I kept the supplies. Of course, he was eager to follow.

When we stood in the corner, I gave him a look of seduction that most men find irresistible. He leaned in for a kiss and I obliged unbuttoning my blouse just enough to be a temptation. It worked because he took me in his arms and deepened the kiss. I held his strong arm as I finished unbuttoning my blouse, slipped out of my skirt, and lay down naked on a bale of hay beckoning him to come and make love to me.

Before you could say "go", he lay down on top of me feeling my body with his rough big hands while kissing my neck. He moved his kisses down my neck and started nibbling that spot right at the bottom that makes me tingle all over. How he knew is beside me. Of course, he could have consulted with some other mates in the area. At any rate, I know rough men have little time for foreplay. He's no different than all the others I've taken to bed. They become so heated at just the sight of me that they want to swallow up my entire body in one bite.

Being accustomed to that, I let him continue biting until his desire overtook him. I was in heaven as we soon became deep in the throes of passion rolling over and over on that big bale of hay, but came back down to earth when an odd feeling came over me. One I have never encountered during casual lovemaking. I opened my eyes right after we finished and sensed that he did not appear to enjoy it as much as I did. I remember thinking how could that be? Any man in his right mind desires my body. I've been compared to the Greek goddess Venus. I realized at that point that he must have had other plans. As he rolled on top of me again, his rough hands moved from caressing my breasts to my neck.

I closed my eyes pretending to be taken with him to see what he was up to. When he thought I was dazed by his lovemaking, he reached for my necklace. He was about to give it a tug when I raised my knee and gave him the most powerful jolt I could, considering my uncompromising position. He fell over into the hay writhing in pain. I scolded him.

"Who do you think you are? I let you romance me, a privilege that should be only for the royal, and you treat me like this? You are nothing more than a conniving thief. Did my unscrupulous but stupid cousins send you?"

He held his masculinity in too much discomfort to respond. When he caught his breath, he answered.

"Yes. Yes, they did. They paid me a bag of gold coins to take it for them."

To say I was livid was an understatement.

"A bag of gold coins? Men would hand over a wagon full just to touch my body let alone make love to me. Now go. Get out of my barn, my manor, and away from me. Let this serve as a lesson to you as well as Thaddeus and Ernest that Amelia once again is smarter than they are and richer since I retained my inheritance. Furthermore, inform them that they can eat their sniveling little hearts out."

Poor Henry was still in so much pain he couldn't get up. That thought alone brought a smile to my face. When he could stand, he ran

69

out of the stable with his pants in his hands much to the wonderment of any staff working in the yard. Those two cousins are despicable beyond words.

My mind snapped back, angry at the cousins' past attempt to get my necklace, but the smile Henry brought me remained on my face. I looked at Madeleine. She seemed confused not only by my sudden appearance but by my expression.

"Madam, are you all right? How long will you be here?"

Duke barked and ran right into my arms. Oh, how I needed his furry love right now. I hugged Duke trying to get him to stop licking my face, but he was so excited to see me that was not possible.

"I will be here two days before I must return. You didn't mention that thief to those two, did you?"

"No. I pray none of us who saw him did. We couldn't bear the thought of working for either of those two greedy callous men."

"That's good. Very good. Since I will be here for such a short time, only you must know of my return. I shall remain hidden in my bedroom closet. Perhaps you could sneak some food and clean clothes to me there?"

Madeleine frowned. "That's such a confined space. Perhaps I can locate a more comfortable one."

"I appreciate your concern, but I must use this location. I can see or hear anything coming through the front door of the manor."

"Very well, Madam. I understand."

We looked at Duke. By now, he was practically doing flips and wagging his tail so fast, I felt a breeze. In this time of unbearable stress, he made us both laugh. "You silly pup," I told him.

Our merriment soon came to an abrupt end when we both heard the thundering hooves of horses in the front yard.

"Quick, my lady. Hide. I fear those wicked men have returned."

I got up, ran back into my closet, and closed the door as tight as I could. Madeleine picked Duke up so he wouldn't follow me and went downstairs. She walked by the various rooms calling out to the other servants to hide. I could hear them scatter in different directions before we all heard a loud and persistent knock echo from the front door. Duke barked. Madeleine still held him while she waited a few seconds before answering. The pounding continued until I heard the heavy wooden front door creak open. I pushed the closet door ajar just enough to hear what was going on. The closet was right off the main hallway, and I needed to know what those miserly cousins wanted. I heard Madeleine's soft voice first.

"My lords, to what do I owe the pleasure of your unexpected visit?"

Thaddeus, my eldest cousin who was tall, lean and I always thought had the jaw of a gorilla, spoke.

"Step aside, washwoman. We want to see the lady of the house and admire her necklace. She has it does she not? We feel she has avoided us long enough."

I could hear my little Duke growl at him from upstairs.

"As I told you a mere two days ago, she left to visit an old friend."

"An old friend … Ha! I don't believe you. You would lie like a rug rather than lose your position. Haven't you heard? We paid a visit to the King."

Madeleine's voice cracked. "The King? Why on earth would he want to see you?"

Thaddeus responded in his gravelly voice. "Madam, the King has great interest in the outcome of this duchy."

"You see we promised his Majesty one third of our rights to this estate for his assistance in obtaining the necklace. He was receptive saying he could always use extra acreage for his children. We told him that Amelia has been nowhere in sight and we feared she fled the country with the necklace or even worse sold it."

71

"The King understood our concern and knew that if she cannot produce that necklace, the duchy and all rights to the royal title reverts back to us."

I could hear Madeleine gasp. "Sirs, you have no right to do this. As I stated, she is on a visit and is wearing the necklace."

I heard a loud slam as Thaddeus pushed Madeline against the wall. She winced in pain.

"Inform your Duchess of this, her time as duchess is coming to an end. I have a scroll under my jacket that is a royal decree from the king himself ordering your mistress to produce her necklace in ten days, or I, being the eldest of us two brothers, shall become the rightful duke and owner of Abbington Manor. I shall nail it to this wall for all who enter and work here to see. Do not think of removing the king's decree or you will find yourself a prisoner of the court."

From the closet, I could hear him pounding nails into the wall. *How could the king fall for such nonsense without attempting to contact me? His actions are not proper. Has he gone mad? Then again, there are many rumors brewing about his failing mind. Those two must have lied to him for His Majesty to decree such an unusual royal decree. Ten days? That shall make my quest all the more difficult now.*

I listened further. Madeleine's voice remained steady and composed in the face of such nasty threats from the cousins.

"I will advise my lady of your visit and your decree immediately upon her return."

"You'd better hope that will be soon or both of you, along with that mangy mutt, will be tossed out homeless into the road."

"I see. Have a pleasant day, my lords."

With that, I heard her slam the door shut. She had to be very angry to behave in that manner. Madeleine was my most trusted servant. If we had been born into similar stations in life, we would be best friends. I soon heard her race up the stairs. Duke followed, scratching at my closet door.

Madeleine opened the door.

"Did you hear all of that rubbish? What on earth will you, will we, do?"

I shook my head.

"Unfortunately, I heard all of it, but why all the pounding?"

"He's a buffoon who wanted to make sure that his point was heard by everyone in the manor. They would then have to ask, and I would have to read them the royal decree. My lady, you have to produce the necklace in ten days or we all must leave the manor."

She began to cry. I stood and hugged her as she pleaded.

"My lady, I don't think I can take any more. What shall we do?"

"Don't worry. I located the necklace and will come back with it before their cowardly deadline. I promise. Now remember, no one must learn of my visit."

She nodded and composed herself before leaving to handle the rest of the servants. I took a deep breath, watching Duke play with his toy, wondering if that was a promise I could keep.

Chapter Seven

I cowered in that tiny closet once Madeleine left with Duke. I heard muted voices but remained afraid to exit. They returned after a short while which for me passed like an eternity. Madeleine carried a tray with shortbread and tea. Duke followed at her heels while she balanced proper clean clothes under one arm. I sighed relieved at the sound of her voice. "My Lady, your tea has arrived. Your cousins are long gone."

No matter how difficult, I knew I had to wait two days before returning to Starr's. Maybe Ryan would know more about Minton by then. Maybe my absence would make him pine for me. I realized I needed to bank my days with Ryan now more than ever, while salivating at the thought of foiling my greedy cousins. The clock was ticking and not in my favor. Madeleine expressed her concern.

"Are you sure you're all right? You carry a great burden. Will my lady be in need of anything else?"

"No. Don't worry. I'm fine, just in need of some rest before Traveling again. I will leave unnoticed the day after tomorrow."

Madeleine curtsied. "It will be my honor to take care of all your needs until then."

With that, she picked Duke up, and left me alone with my thoughts. I tried hard to get Ryan, Minton, and now my devious cousins, out of my mind but couldn't. I fell asleep curled up against the closet wall until the bold morning light streaming beneath the door and aroused me from a dream.

I jolted awake when I heard the sounds of heavy footsteps coming up the grand staircase. I heard Duke barking from another room and Madeleine's irritated voice from this one.

"But sirs, as I told you yesterday, she is not here. Why don't you believe me?"

Ernest answered, "Because Amelia is as cunning as a fox."

It was the cousins again. They sounded more determined than yesterday so out of caution, I exited the closet and pushed on the left side of the large bookcase opposite my bed. It rotated until a secret compartment opened. I quickly darted inside, closing the heavy case behind me. The footsteps approached the bedroom door before stopping. I heard Madeleine enter the room again after I left and try to lock the door behind her.

Thaddeus spoke first.

"Washwoman, you know I threatened to cut off one of the other servants' hands before he informed me that he heard Amelia's voice coming from this very room yesterday. George, your oh so loyal gardener, swore on his wife's grave, after I choked him just enough, that he heard Amelia's voice coming from an upstairs window again today. Since we are upstairs, open this door now or your own fate will prove as nasty."

I heard Madeleine's voice waiver.

"Yes, sirs."

Their hefty footsteps vibrated in the room. The cousins were loud, shouting as they turned drawers upside down and threw my books on the floor. I heard them walk over to my closet. Madeleine gasped as they pulled the door open.

"She's not in there. I already stated she is with a friend."

Her voice quivered, surprised by my absence. I realized all too well I must leave straightaway. I called on Starr one day early hoping she

75

would understand, hoping it would not interfere with the winds. I wanted my plan to remain intact hoping she would hear my whispers.

"Starr present. Spare me from my cousins' greed. Starr present. Starr present."

I waited in silence, only to hear their gruff voices again.

"We'll search this entire manor. We will turn things upside down until we find her hiding place and that necklace. Do you understand?"

I heard Madeleine cry out.

"Yes, my lords, but she and her necklace are not here."

I sank down in a dark spot waiting for the winds. I felt cold and trembled from the fear of being found.

I wanted to cry as I heard the cousins throwing my most precious possessions around, shattering some into pieces.

A nasty voice echoed through the walls.

"Nothing here, Thaddeus. We've searched this entire room. That excuse for a royal must be wearing our family's necklace. Let's search the woods for her. I have a feeling she may be close by."

Madeleine squealed as they shoved her aside. Their heavy footsteps stomped down the stairs before the two men slammed the front door shut.

I couldn't believe my ears. Just in time! I heard the strong sounds of those winds approach. Fearing I could still be discovered, I didn't move a muscle.

Without warning, they picked me up where I sat and swirled me around. Their robust gusts moved the bookcase and blew the secret passageway open before lifting me high into the clouds. I was deathly afraid to open my eyes for fear of falling. After I calmed down, I spread my arms out wide, drifting back and forth like a hawk in flight spinning me around over the very forest my cousins searched. I became dizzy until *clunk!* I landed hard in the middle of Starr's reading room. I had trouble catching my breath and doubled over before looking up.

"I have never been so happy to see anyone in my life."

Starr was standing over me, arms crossed. "What do you mean? Spare you from your greedy cousins? Why? What happened?"

"By royal decree, I must return with the necklace nine days hence or surrender my duchy. They were tearing my manor apart searching for me. Two separate ungrateful servants told them they heard my voice. Imagine, after all I do for them. Are those conniving earls able to follow me here?"

Starr remained silent.

"Only if they have a skilled seer. Do they?"

"They may be monsters but stupid ones at that."

Starr expressed concern. "Nine days to return with the necklace. That's quite a feat, even for you. You now have seven days here. Will you ask Mr. Redstone about his contact? As luck will have it, he's due for an appointment in fifteen minutes. You have consumed his mind, making it difficult for me to introduce him to any women. Now go change and freshen up please."

Fifteen minutes? I was exhausted from Travel, but the thought of meeting Ryan made me race upstairs to make myself desirable if that's possible in Starr's limited wardrobe. Ryan knocked on Starr's front door just as I finished dressing. I overheard Starr's greeting.

"Ryan, please come in. Let's go to my reading room where I can answer your questions about all the lovely ladies I found for you."

Lovely ladies? What was Starr doing? I needed to hurry and make myself known before she diverted his attention to someone else. I scampered down the stairs and cut them off in the hallway.

Ryan's gaze revealed everything I needed to know about his feelings for me. His eyes lit up like shooting stars as they filled with happiness. My surprise rendered him speechless. "Mr. Redstone. What a pleasant surprise Maybe we could talk about that necklace after you meet with Starr?"

Ryan nodded affirmative as he took my hand and squeezed it.

The gypsy's eyes shot daggers at me before she interrupted.

"That will be fine, but our meeting may take quite a while, Amy. I have a lot of lovely ladies to show Mr. Redstone. Maybe you should think about reading or taking a walk while you wait."

Now my eyes shot daggers right back at Starr. The gypsy grabbed Ryan's hand from mine and whisked him away into the reading room. Just before Starr commandeered him, Ryan winked and leaned in to whisper in hushed tones. "Amy, meet me outside in an hour near my car, or should I say my carriage? You can't imagine how much I've missed you."

I blew him a kiss before he entered the reading room. Starr closed the door behind them.

Once outside, my eyes searched for his carriage. I sat on a bench not too far from it, removing a small hourglass from my skirt pocket. I had played with it in my closet to pass the time and brought it with me by accident. I wished the sands of time were as speedy as those winds. Just before the last few grains passed through, I heard a welcome familiar voice.

"Amy, I missed you! Would you like to go back to the riverfront and continue our discussion?"

I was delighted by his invitation.

"What a delicious idea!"

Ryan opened the side door. Eager, I got in.

"So tell me. How many beautiful women did Starr show you?"

Ryan chuckled. "Why? Are you jealous?"

"Silly boy ... not a chance."

"Okay. There were four."

"And you decided to meet one?"

"I said I would have to think about it. I've been thinking of you the whole time. You're hard to forget."

I was delighted to hear that. "I have been thinking of you, as well."

It didn't take long for his carriage to reach the riverfront. We stopped in front of his guest house, a two level building. Ryan leaned over and kissed my cheek, whispering in my ear, "Please let's go back to my room. It's just upstairs. You can tell me what your secret is in private. I trust you and hope you trust me."

Ryan helped me out of his carriage. We climbed the one flight of steps up to his room. Once inside, I saw a poorly decorated drab gray room with a double bed. I walked over, sat down on the bed and stared out the large single window before giving him a serious look.

"This is not how I planned to tell you. I hoped to wait until we saw if the necklace was genuine. You must listen to me before passing judgment. I hope you will still want to keep me in your heart afterward."

Ryan walked by closing the drapes before sitting down next to me.

"Amy, how could I help but keep you in my heart, no matter what your secret is?"

He squeezed my hand as I touched his lips with the softest of kisses. Just Ryan's touch filled me with the deepest passion. I kissed his hand ready to reveal my desire for him especially since I now knew he felt the same way. I wanted to show him my love in a special manner. Standing up, I slowly removed Starr's silk floral sash and placed it around his neck. I moved in close to him and he kissed my waist.

I jumped back pulling the sash to dance the seductive dance of the gypsy women who camped outside my childhood manor house grounds. They always looked so graceful, silver bracelets jingling, ribbon colored skirts twirling as they turned and twisted by their campfire in the moonlight. They seduced traveling knights and lesser royals, hoping for romantic trysts, out of their coin. I had heard the gypsies' haunting songs and desired to get a better look. I became quite good at sneaking out night after night, hoping not to get caught. Hiding in some nearby bushes, I watched them dance. One night, a beautiful gypsy spotted my hiding place and grabbed me. To my surprise, she had me stand and taught me their dance.

I wanted to get my necklace back, but strange as it sounds, I wanted Ryan more. I unbuttoned my blouse, removing it first, and touching his face with its soft perfumed silk. I swirled around pulling my camisole off and throwing it on the ground. I danced back to him close enough for him to kiss my breasts. I turned to kick off my shoes before stepping out of my petticoats and skirt one layer at a time. I continued to seduce him, taking off each undergarment until I stripped myself bare. His face flushed with passion. He seemed reluctant at first but finally gave into his feelings. He stared longingly at my naked body, his eyes intoxicated by passion. I have been with enough men to know he liked what he saw.

I danced naked back to where he could touch me. He leaned into me kissing my waist before moving his wet lips from my abdomen to my shoulder. I was aroused like never before. I couldn't stand my body's anticipation any longer. Taking his hands off my waist, I pulled him up and helped him disrobe. His naked body was a feast for my eyes; he was as muscular as a bull. I moved in and caressed him so our bodies touched every part of the other's. Our body heat was so intense, we could have started a fire. We soon lay down together on the bed.

His hands were smooth with a gentle touch, making my body desire him all the more. I wanted to feel his touch and warm kisses on every part of my body. I turned and moved so he could make that happen. His kisses lingered and became more intense with each turn. He held my wrists to stop my turning before he lay on top of me. We made sweet love until we became so tired, we both fell asleep. Our nap was all too brief.

Ryan was the first to wake up. He whispered my name, "Amy, my love, wake up sweetheart."

He kissed me awake. I stretched, remembering where I was and what I needed to tell him. My feelings for him now made it more complicated than ever. I sat up.

"Ryan, please listen. I must tell you about me right now."

"Okay. I'm all yours especially after this afternoon."

He raised his right hand in the air. "I promise to be open to anything you have to tell me…"

He sat on the edge of the bed next to me. I swallowed hard and took his hand.

"The first thing I should tell you is that I'm a Traveler."

He appeared a bit puzzled, "A Traveler. You mean a tourist?"

"No. I'm a Time Traveler. I have Traveled here from 1761, to be exact. I needed to consult with Starr about a problem that has to be resolved in your present."

Ryan laughed. "You silly girl. More humor. What an imagination! I told you that you should write stories. I love that about you. If we had more time I'd show you just how much."

I looked more serious this time.

"I am not kidding. Starr, besides finding true love, brings Travelers to the present to resolve any issues that another Traveler with bad intentions may have brought to this time. Do you understand all that? I know it must sound like total rubbish, but it is the truth. I never expected to fall so head over heels in love with you. I thought about you, day and night since our very first meeting. I thought you might help me get my inheritance back, but now I realize I must not involve you and take care of this myself. I have encountered new obstacles and will never forgive myself if I put the love of my life in harm's way."

"The love of your life? I'm honored, and I'm beginning to think the same about you. Your inheritance? I'm baffled."

Ryan answered in a soft tone not knowing how to take this new information.

"Yes, my love, my inheritance. I am as of 1753 the rightful Duchess of Abbington. That necklace in the drawing is mine passed down from an understanding king. Whoever has possession of the necklace has possession of the manor house, the title, and everything that goes with it."

He looked at me, studying my expressions.

"You look like you're telling the truth. You look like the woman in the drawing. How did the necklace end up with that guy in Miami?"

"You mean Minton. He's a Traveler as well, not affiliated with Starr, who came back to my time with deceitful intentions. As I told you before, he said he wanted to examine the necklace to reproduce copies for sale. He caught me off guard, stole it, killing one of my most trusted guards in the process, before he was called to the present. He intended to sell the necklace and get rich. I am determined to get my inheritance back from the scoundrel, no matter what it takes."

"I don't know what to believe." Ryan leaned in and kissed my cheek.

"He may have stolen your necklace, but you've stolen my heart. That has not happened to me for a long time. I want to believe you but don't know if I should. This is a confusing dilemma. I need time to think."

I stood up and started dressing before walking over to the window. I pushed the drapes to the side just enough to look out.

"Ryan, my love. There's nothing you need to do except show me who this man is and where I can see the necklace."

"After you see it, what will you do?"

I was reluctant to tell him my plan. I knew that must remain my problem. He hesitated.

"I'm not sure about that yet. I want you to be safe so I'll tell you once I decide. There is one thing I am sure of, and that is I have fallen in love with you."

I walked back to Ryan, who had finished dressing, and kissed him. He looked at his watch and felt for something in his pocket.

"Oh no! My phone, where is it?"

"Phone? What's a phone?"

"Please don't joke. That man is supposed to call me two hours from now with details of the necklace. I must have left it at Starr's. I'll call her to see if she found it."

He touched the keys on a small black box on the nightstand. I noticed Starr had a few of these odd looking devices in her home. One was even on my bed stand. I could hear Starr answer.

"Starr Knight making dreams come true. How may I help you?"

"Starr, it's Ryan. I think I left my cell there. Did you find it?"

"You left it in the reading room under those bios I prepared for you."

Starr laughed. "Guess you forgot those as well."

Ryan was so relived he shot me a wink.

"You found it! Thank goodness! I'm on my way. Give me about forty-five minutes. Sorry to trouble you. If you have someone there just place it on the front hall table. Thanks."

"It's all right. I don't have any more appointments today. Come when you can."

Ryan hung up and looked at me. I couldn't help my curiosity.

"Tell me, Ryan, what do these devices do?"

"They are called phones, silly. Is this another of your jokes? You can call out by touching the numbers on the base here or you can listen to a conversation through this part of the phone."

He picked up what looked like a black handle and held it to his ear to demonstrate.

"Starr's phones are all connected so you can hear any conversation from any extension as they are called. Now enough questions. We must hurry, darling. We have to get there as soon as possible. I can't miss that call."

He went into the small commode, washed his face, and combed his hair. I tidied my appearance in the dresser mirror. Ryan looked at me and bowed.

"My lady, your horseless carriage awaits."

Chapter Eight

As we approached Starr's, I informed Ryan I thought it best if she did not see us together. A wise lad, he dropped me off at the end of the gypsy's street. Before I left the carriage, he gave me careful instructions.

"I don't understand why I want to help you. Your Time Travel story is hard for me to swallow, but the funny thing is love makes you blind. I love you and want to help you. Meet me at the Egg House tomorrow for lunch. Say about noon. I should have some news by then."

I gave him a quick kiss, stepped out of his carriage, and walked the four blocks back to Starr's. Ryan arrived ahead of me. I used the key Starr gave me to sneak in the back door. I hid in the front hall behind a large fern off to one side and not in their direct view. Starr and Ryan were already seated in her reading room.

"Ryan, I'm always glad to see you. I found your phone here on the table. You must have been in a hurry because you left these as well."

Starr handed him the bios of the other women she selected for him. Oh, how I'd love to rush in there and rip those papers up. I peeked inside.

Ryan appeared relieved as the gypsy opened her mahogany sideboard drawer and took out a small black object. She handed it to him.

"Thanks. You're a lifesaver. That man with the necklace is supposed to call me in an hour."

Starr offered to make him coffee.

"You're most welcome to wait here. Maybe we could look at a few more photos while you wait? I'll bring out some coffee and my special cherry vanilla cupcakes."

I'm quite sure she favored the other women for my Ryan because she must be afraid I would hurt him. I was not surprised by that, considering my past. Since I had an hour to wait, I tiptoed upstairs to take a quick rinsing, change my clothes, and prepare the pistol I hid in my nightstand drawer during my visit. This particular English dueling pistol was made for my uncle in London. It had exquisitely carved wooden handles with a small brass plate showing the duke's personal crest. Since my father taught me to shoot, I did not fear using it. I Traveled last time carrying it in my pocket along with a velvet pouch containing the round bullets, flint, and my thin cleaning tools.

Starr has always been considerate of her guests' privacy. So I was never concerned she would search my room.

I sat on the edge of the bed, towel drying my hair while daydreaming about my sweet revenge. I opened the drawer and held the pistol firmly in my hand. I never advocated violence, but I knew only an act of desperation would get my necklace back and reclaim my title. It had been a donkey's years since I last fired it.

We had problems at home last year with wolves killing our sheep. Luckily for me, I recently had Donny, my most trusted stable hand, refresh my memory as to how to load the pistol with proper form. I stared in the mirror aiming the pistol.

"Minton, you will now do as I say. Give me back my necklace."

I was amazed at how stern I sounded and how prepared I was to kill that scoundrel. My thoughts quickly shifted.

"Now my sweet Ryan, all you have to do is take me to Minton and leave. My love for you will not allow me to involve you in my problem."

I put the pistol back in the drawer and stepped outside my room. Standing at the top of the stairs, I saw Ryan and Starr laughing just as his pocket device buzzed. I could hear their conversation.

"Excuse me, Starr. I don't mean to interrupt, but I should take this call. It could be Minton."

Starr reached for his hand and nodded.

Ryan stepped out into the hallway right under the upstairs landing. His device continued to buzz.

I crept down a few stairs when I heard Ryan answer.

"Redstone here."

Ryan walked around changing the position of his device as he did. By his expression, I could see he was having difficulty hearing. He walked out the front door for a few minutes before returning.

"Minton, you are breaking up. I can barely hear you. Would you mind if I called you back from a landline?"

Ryan continued to pace around Starr's front hall as he spoke. "Give me five minutes to get near a phone. Can you still hear me? Okay. I'll call you right back."

Ryan clicked the button on his small device and called out to Starr. She came racing out.

"Ryan, is everything all right?"

"Not exactly. My phone battery must have run out. I foolishly left my charger in my hotel room. May I please call Minton back from one of your phones? I will pay for any charges."

Starr was quick to respond.

"Yes, of course, whatever you need. Come, there's one in the parlor."

He followed Starr into her parlor. Once he was inside, she slid the wooden doors closed and left. *What shall I do now?*

Just then I remembered what Ryan said about being able to hear from any of the boxes. I had one in my room so I got up and raced into my bedroom. I was quiet picking up that odd looking handle with care.

I first heard Ryan.

"Is this better?"

I then heard that familiar yet conniving voice respond.

"Yes much. Minton, here. I have the necklace in my possession. I can't show it to you tomorrow, but Thursday afternoon would work for me. When it meets your appraisal for authenticity, we will make the deal. Money and necklace to change hands at the same time."

That absolute scoundrel! I'd love to yell into this foolish thing and tell him what I think of him. I refrained, knowing better if I wanted to regain possession of my jewels.

Ryan replied without hesitation. "Of course, Mr. Minton. Thursday is fine. You remember we discussed that our board of directors must approve my appraisal before any funds are given out. Would two in the afternoon work for you? That will give me enough time to find you."

"That would be fine," Minton answered. "I am in the Seybold Building in the Jewelry Mart. Do you know where that is?"

Ryan responded. "Please hold on. I need to get a pen and paper to write that down. Okay, the Seybold Building? No, I don't know where that is, but I have a GPS in my rental car if you give me the street address and number."

"No problem. We are at 36 NE 1st Street in Miami. I look forward to our meeting on Thursday. I'll be there at two on the dot."

I heard a clicking sound and no more voices. I put the handle back on the box before anyone knew I used it. I went back to the top of the stairs just as Ryan called out for Starr."

"Starr, thank you very much."

"Not a problem. Did your call go through okay?"

"Yes, it did, and we arranged for a meeting."

"Well, I hope all goes well for you."

"Me too."

With that, Ryan left. He walked outside to his rental car, as he called it, and drove off. I would not see him again until the next day. I didn't know if my heart could last that long.

~ * ~

Noon on Wednesday took an eternity to arrive. I walked with anticipation to The Egg House. I passed by all the diners chatting while my eyes searched for my love.

There he is! I spotted Ryan waiting in his carriage across the way. His face erupted into a large grin when he saw me cross the street. I rushed over, got in, and kissed him on the cheek.

"Did that scoundrel reach you?"

I asked even though I knew the answer.

"He sure did. Mr. Minton called asking to meet in Miami at two tomorrow afternoon to show me the necklace."

"You will go, won't you?"

"Of course. I have to, for work. The necklace is the reason I'm here, remember?"

I laughed. "I thought I was. May I could come along?"

"You are determined, aren't you? Maybe, but only if I think it safe. Aren't you concerned he'll recognize you?"

"Not if I promise to keep a low profile. I have to see if that necklace is really mine."

Ryan remained silent for a few seconds.

"I'll say yes, even though it's against my better judgment. You'll have to sit and wait for me in the car. We'll leave from here, the café, around eleven. That should give me enough time to locate the building. Meet me here ten minutes before."

I threw my arms around him and hugged him as tight as I could.

"You are my hero. My knight in shining armor. Now, I don't know about you, but I have the rest of the day free. This is day two of my seven days, so let's make the most of it."

Ryan kissed me. "Okay then, let's do something special. Would you like to see the beach? We could take a ride out to Sanibel Island and have dinner by the water."

I clapped happy at that thought.

"Sounds delightful. Any chance of finishing the evening back at your room?"

Chapter Nine

We ate dinner that night at a beautiful blue house on the water. Ryan ordered a fish called snapper for both of us and it was most delicious. It is difficult to get such a fresh fish dinner where I live. I'm such a long carriage ride from the coast. We chatted about everything, our lives, our pets, our dreams. I have never connected with a man in that way before. After dinner, we walked outside the restaurant to watch the sun set. Many other patrons followed. Ryan said it was a tradition on this small peaceful island. We kissed when the last rays of the sun disappeared under the water and a flash of green light appeared.

"Amy, now that you've seen Sanibel's famous green flash, let's take a walk along the beach." We walked under the light of a full moon stopping at one of the beach houses for let that had a park bench that faced the water. Ryan turned and looked into my eyes.

"Amy, please come here and sit with me. I'm sure no-one will mind."

Once seated next to Ryan, I watched as he took a small velvet box from his pocket. He opened it to reveal a ring with a tiny blue stone in the center of a gold rose.

He took the ring out and held it in his hand before looking into my eyes.

"Amy, I love you. This ring belonged to my great Aunt Beth. She died a year ago, and told me before she did to give this to the next

90

woman who steals my heart. Aunt Beth said I needed the companionship of a good woman. She was right because that, my love, is you. I know it's not a diamond but the deep blue of this sapphire reflects the depth of my love."

He took my hand and placed the ring on my left ring finger.

Tears of joy streamed down my face… tears of joy… not frustration, or anger, or from being insulted. He said I was a good woman. I've heard tart, bawdy, disgraceful, but never good. *Oh, Ryan you truly are the man of my dreams.*

He kissed me before we left for his carriage. I felt like a school girl with her first crush. How wonderful!

After I left Ryan that evening, I experienced great difficulty falling asleep. Thoughts of falling in love, committing murder, and staving off my terrible cousins consumed my mind, making me toss and turn like a schooner in a storm. Should I give up my title for Ryan and desert my manor staff? I thought of Madeleine and our close bond not to mention the other families whom I promised to care for.

When morning arrived, my first thoughts were of Ryan and the most romantic evening of my life. Good thing Starr gave me a set of keys, making it easy for me to sneak in and out of here. Then reality struck and struck me hard. I was on Day Three. I had to resolve this as soon as possible or I shall vanish into thin air. Problems awaited me at home, especially if I returned without my necklace. Today was my best chance of getting close to Minton and carrying out my plan.

I hurried my dress, selecting a high collared lilac blouse and a layered skirt in shades of purple with deep pockets, perfect for hiding my weapon. Cautious, I cleaned my pistol before loading it.

Minton will have no choice but to hand over my inheritance. His life will rest in my hands. Ryan must not be a part of this in any way. Minton will know he's dealing with me and me alone. I hope not to scare Ryan off. I have never felt this way about any man before. He is more important than my mission, proof I must take care of this myself.

I searched the dresser drawers in my room and found one of Starr's black velvet evening purses. Having a drawstring close, I found it perfect to place my extra bullets in. As I walked downstairs, Starr encouraged me with a cheerful greeting.

"Amelia, you look lovely, those shades suit you. They bring out the color of your eyes. You are glowing. Have you any news about your necklace?"

I hesitated hating to lie to Starr. I crossed my fingers on my right hand and placed them behind me. I was told that negates the lie.

"No, no news."

"Well, don't give up. Something good will happen. I can feel it. What's this? A sapphire ring. What a lovely setting. More from your jewelers? I must Travel back to your time and buy myself some jewelry."

She took my hand to get a better look. "Why is it on you left hand?"

Good thing I was not born with beauty alone but a quick wit.

"Because I wish to discourage any potential suitors."

Starr laughed. "You sure have had enough of them. Where are you off to today?"

"I'd thought I'd do a little window shopping to pass the time."

"Do you need some current money? After all, you gave me all those gold pieces. Here let me get you some."

Starr walked over to her purse on the hall table and took out four paper bills, each marked twenty.

"Here's eighty dollars. Hope you find something you like."

"Why, thank you. I'm sure I will."

I did not want Starr to suspect I was up to something other than shopping. Hopefully, I gave nothing away. Starr started to ask another question but hesitated. I guess she decided to pass, not wanting a confrontation about Ryan. I took the twenties and put them in the velvet bag.

"I'll see you later. Do you have clients today?"

"Why, yes, I have two."

"Well then, all the best romance hunting."

With that remark, I opened the large wooden front door and left for The Egg House. I glanced at my watch. I was half an hour early. I must be excited at the thought of seeing Ryan and my necklace, both in one day. I quickened my pace until my handsome Ryan came into view, eating a full breakfast. I snuck up behind him and surprised him.

"Now that's a proper breakfast." I giggled.

"Hey beautiful, let me order you one."

"No, I'm not hungry. I'm a bit anxious about seeing my inheritance again. We need to talk."

Ryan placed his toast back on his plate. "Sure honey, what's wrong?"

"I need to know that no matter what today brings, you'll still love me and believe in me. No matter what, that will not change."

"Amy, honey, of course I love you, and I do believe you. You are the first woman since Jillian's death I could love and now you have my ring as well as my heart. Don't get so nervous. We don't know if this guy is even for real. He could just be a scam artist. I've read there are plenty of them in Florida."

He took a few more bites of his bacon. I was reluctant to ask but needed to know his answer.

"If you had to choose between me and your job and current life, which would it be?"

"Do you think I'd ever have to make that choice?"

I answered coyly. "I'll have to go back soon. Time Travel is rough on a body, besides, I'll have to resolve an annoying issue at home. By

Travelers' Rules, I may not be able to return once this matter is resolved."

Ryan sat back. "Ah yes, your Time Travel. Let's deal with that when we have to. But now, it's time for us to travel to Miami."

He laughed before gulping down the rest of his meal and paid his bill.

"Come on let's get going."

He grabbed my arm and walked me to his carriage. Once seated inside, I watched Ryan press some buttons on another peculiar device in the front of the carriage. He decided to tell me about it before I asked.

"This is a GPS. It speaks directions. Today is a very important day for each of us, so we want to make sure we can find this man." Ryan started the carriage and off we went. We spoke little on the way to Miami. I thought he was pondering my odd questions; I wondered what choices he would make when today came to an end.

I saw a sign by the road that read Alligator Alley. I hoped we would not come in contact with any. I had read how dangerous they were.

Ryan looked over at me. "Amy, you know you really do worry too much. This guy could be an imposter with a fake necklace."

"I don't think so. I do believe he is the man who stole it."

"I guess I do too. I just wanted you to feel better. Okay, we're almost there. The GPS is telling me to turn. I have to pay attention to find this Seybold Building."

The woman's voice coming from the little box guided us making us turn left and then right until we rode right past our destination. Ryan backtracked a little, made a U-turn as he called it, and found a parking space not too far away from the correct building.

We stopped, but Ryan didn't get out. Instead, he turned my face toward him with his hand.

"Now, you must pay strict attention to me. I'll go in first by myself. I will find Minton and ask that he show me the necklace. I'll look at the necklace with my jeweler's eyepiece to try and find the maker's mark. Remember, I can't pay for it today so you might as well be patient and just wait here, if that's even possible. I'll leave the air conditioning or should I say cool air on with the keys in the ignition like this. I will tell you what I think when I get back. Okay?"

I refused to answer; I just shot a sweet smile. Above all else, I am a lady of my word for important things and I did not want to agree to something I couldn't do. Ryan got out and started to walk over to The Seybold Building. I watched through the side mirror of the carriage to make sure he went inside the main entrance before getting out. I paced myself.

I thought I'd better take these keys for fear a total stranger might drive off with Ryan's carriage. This time and place seems to attract thieves. I'd like to run inside and face Minton, but I don't want to give my plan up.

I stepped out of the carriage and looked around. There was no one in view so I stopped and hid behind a short full palm. The main floor of the building had floor to ceiling windows. I moved so that I was able to watch through one of them just in time to see Ryan enter a cubicle through some kind of magical door that opened by itself. I waited, giving him enough time to locate Minton. He never told me the precise location of Minton's business, let alone what level. I walked inside, spotting a large sign with many names until I found that scurrilous name—Minton.

Minton, Stuart, 3rd floor, Suite 316. *Well, Mr. Minton, we are about to meet again.*

I was more than a bit unsure of using the large cubicle I heard going up and down, but I found the staircase and climbed to the "Third Floor." As I opened the door from the stairwell, I saw that the numbers nearest the door were 320 and 319 so I followed them to 316. All the enclosures had a large glass window facing the walk. I peaked in Minton's window and saw Ryan. I couldn't believe my eyes! He was holding and examining my necklace. Imagine that! I could still see fine strands of my hair on it. Minton must have kept it hidden, waiting for Ryan's museum to buy it.

I jumped to the side of the window to keep my plan a surprise for a few more seconds, then peered carefully inside again. I lost it when I saw Minton pick the necklace up and start to put it in my very own velvet jewelry pouch. My blood boiled as I watched that evil man walk my inheritance back to his large open safe. I unbuttoned the top of my blouse. This time, I guess you could say it was for my benefit. I pulled my pistol out of my pocket, ready to kill him. Bursting into Minton's office, I pointed the barrel of my gun directly at his heart. I was so angry all I could do was shout at him.

"You scoundrel! You murderous thief! Thought you saw the end of the likes of me, huh? Well, you are wrong. Stop. Do not lock that bag away. I demand you hand me my necklace right now!"

I stared Minton in the eyes. He was so stunned, it was as if he saw a ghost. The man couldn't move a muscle. Ha, he did not know about Starr and must not have expected me to Travel. Minton turned his conniving gaze to Ryan.

"Mr. Redstone, I assure you that I have no idea who this crazy woman is and what she could possibly want with me."

Ryan appeared just as stunned as Minton. Aiming the barrel of my pistol directly at Minton's heart, I steadied it with both hands, placing one finger on the trigger, ready to fire.

"Let me see if I can jog your memory? Oh yes, you wanted me to help you learn the art of jewelry making from my time. You must be a quick study, not of jewelry making but of stealing and murder. You do remember killing my guard, or has that left your memory along with my identity, as well?"

I was slow and methodical as I pushed the pistol closer to Minton. I wanted to savor every minute of this. Just the sight of the man made me sick. I let him into my manor and my bed and this is how he treated me. I noticed he was quick to reach under the counter.

"If you move your hands one more time, I'll have to shoot you on the spot. I am a skilled marksman so trust me I shan't miss. Now, hold both hands in the air where I can see them."

His face paled as if drained of blood as he raised his arms in the air. I wanted him to know how much he hurt me. I wanted him to be terrified of me. I moved in close enough to shove the pistol into Minton's jugular. Looking into his beady eyes, I warned him.

"You have no idea how much I'd like to pull the trigger right now."

As I spoke, Ryan tried to intervene.

"Amy, please. This is not necessary. Don't shoot him. You'll only be hurting yourself. If you're sure that's your necklace, just take it and leave him alone."

Minton was shaking, afraid to speak on his own behalf. Tears streamed down his cheeks. *Coward!* My weapon still poised at his throat, his hands shook, trying to clutch the velvet bag as tight as he could. I kept my eyes on Minton while addressing Ryan.

"I told you earlier that you might have to make a choice today. When I leave this store, you will have to think about those questions I asked earlier. No matter what you decide, remember I love you and always will. This scoundrel may have stolen my necklace but you stole my heart"

Minton squirmed, trying to get his neck away from my pistol. No chance of that.

"Well, Mr. Stuart Minton, it appears the wind is now at my back. You stay still. Very still. Wouldn't want my hands to shake and pull the trigger in error. That would be a pity. Now hand over my necklace … or should I ask you to disrobe first?"

Minton appeared even paler than before for one with such a tanned complexion. He realized I would shoot him as easily as a squirrel on the hunting trail. He decided to do exactly what I asked and handed over my velvet bag. I peeked inside to make sure that he didn't remove the necklace and con me again.

"Don't think of coming after me. I know you have a seer who can take you back to my time, but let me tell you that everyone in my duchy knows who you are and that you killed my most trusted guard. They will seek you out and kill you like a pheasant for Sunday dinner."

Minton remained stunned but listened. After all, I still had the pistol pointed to his throat. Ryan looked at me, his pleading eyes trying to get me to reconsider my actions.

"Amy, you don't have to get the necklace back this way."

"Yes, I do. I have no choice. I suppose I could call the authorities but would they really believe my story? Somehow I don't think so."

Minton moved to the side a few inches.

"Minton, stand still. As for killing my guard, I should kill you, but I won't stoop to your level."

Deep in my heart, I knew I couldn't kill him in front of the man I loved. I took five slow steps back from Minton, who breathed a deep sigh of relief.

"I won't kill you, but I will nick you just to make sure you stay put."

I fired my pistol, shattering his knee. He fell to the ground, bleeding and writhing in pain.

Ryan looked stunned by this turn of events. I stared into his eyes.

"I have to go back now before the present authorities come for me. I'm sorry you had to be a witness to this. You can reach me through Starr. I love you, Ryan. My love for you is genuine and forever. Goodbye."

I kissed Ryan before rushing out into the hallway and slamming the door shut. Minton must have managed to pull an alarm of sorts when I ran. From the corner of my eye, I saw him reach under his counter. When I heard the blaring noise of his siren, I knew I had to act fast. I went out into the stairway and looked up at the sky and called out.

"Starr, past. Starr, past. Starr, past… Send me home."

I knew those special winds could take hours to get me. I ran down the stairs and outside. I continued running until I was out of sight of the building escaping into an alley near the rear of the adjacent building. I was out of breath and exhausted, but could not stop until I was safe. I did not hear the winds but carriages with lights and sirens come to a screeching halt in front of Minton's address.

Men in dark blue uniforms jumped out of three vehicles.

"We have to find her. The victim said the thief was in her thirties with light brown hair and iris-colored eyes. Remember he said she was dangerous and out of her mind claiming to be from the 1700's. Minton said she was armed and shot him. If she approaches and points her gun at you, do not, I repeat, do not be afraid to fire your weapon. If she threatens your life in any way, make that a kill shot. Okay, let's go find her and bring her in with the jewels."

I peered around the side of the building watching the men disperse in all directions. What shall I do? Where are those bloody winds?

I heard one of them shout, "There she is. I can see her behind the building next door. Back up needed. Approach with extreme caution."

I still held the pistol in my right hand while holding the necklace with my other. I placed the pistol in my skirt pocket and held onto my necklace with all my might. It didn't take long for those men to surround the building. I was cornered like a fox on the hunting trail. Just when I thought my escape was foiled, I heard that familiar yet eerie whooshing sound of the winds. What impeccable timing! They swept me up where I stood just as those men were closing in. They saw me go up in the cyclone of air. One shouted at the top of his lungs.

"Did you see that? How did she do that? Is she a magician or have some kind of air machine?"

Another guardsman fired his weapon at me but I was too high for any of his bullets to hit me.

"How do we explain this to the chief? Don't think I want that job." I drifted up and down like a hawk in flight. I felt a bit dizzy before the winds steadied my Travel. I swooped down a bit to get one last look at my love. There he was, a gentleman wrapping Minton's leg with his shirt to ease the bleeding. I hovered to watch through the glass front window before I swirled by. He looked up and saw me. His eyes were sad—very sad. I'm quite sure he found it hard to believe his eyes let alone the fact that I had left him. I saw him mouth some words through the glass.

"Amy, I'll help you. Please don't go … don't go" were the last words I saw him speak before being whirled around at top speed in that cyclone of time. I cried my heart out at the thought of leaving him. The speed of the wind dried my tears. I spun around and around before I slowed and crash landed with a loud thump back at Abbington Manor.

Relieved, I clutched that black velvet bag as I found myself lying on my red Chinese rug while looking around at the all too comforting surroundings of my drawing room. Duke must have heard me fall and came running in to greet me. I picked him up. I laughed as he wouldn't stop licking my face. My laugh did not last long as I thought of what lie ahead with my cousins and what my life would be like without Ryan.

Chapter Ten

Madeleine was in the next room and heard my loud return. She rushed in, surprised to find me lying there with Duke in my arms licking my face. I could tell she had a difficult time in my absence. Her skin was pale; her eyes tired. She became animated by my presence.

"Why, my lady, how did you enter without me seeing you? Where were you? You were gone for more days than expected. Others noticed your absence and became concerned about your safety as well. After all, you are a woman traveling alone with no knight. Your angry cousins have been here every day demanding to see you. I kept them at bay as best I could."

Madeleine walked over to me. "Please, my lady, allow me to help you up."

She carefully took my arm and helped me stand. I was a bit shaky from Travel and the events that preceded it. Duke remained in my arms. He continued to lick my face like he thought he'd never see me again. Madeleine laughed as she watched him. Her eyes became huge as she took in my exposed ankles and shocking manner of dress.

"Please, my lady, let me take you upstairs to your room and help you bathe and dress properly. I don't know where you find such scandalous attire."

"Thank you, Madeleine. Once we have finished, please have Simon notify my concerned cousins to come for a visit so I may show them my necklace."

"Yes, my lady. Straightaway. Did I hear you say your necklace? How wonderful! Arthur's killer had it, didn't he? Did he meet with appropriate justice? You risked your own life to catch him."

"We shall never see him again. I took care of that, but I never considered my own safety. I wanted the scoundrel who killed Arthur to suffer. I found him and shot his leg. He had my necklace. I took it back, while telling him that if he ever showed his face at Abbington Manor again, he would be a dead man."

Madeleine gasped. "My lady, you are so brave! Now that you're safe at home, how about a nice cup of tea and some homemade biscuits after your bath? You must be exhausted. Some rest will help before dealing with those horrible cousins of yours."

Madeleine escorted me up to my bedroom. Duke followed at my heels. I lay on the bed, tired from the stress of chasing Minton, tired from Time Travel, but happy to be home. Duke jumped up for another hug. I was only too happy to oblige. Madeleine left to go to the kitchen to heat water on the fire for my bath.

I hugged Duke again before opening my velvet bag. I took out my necklace and held it in my hands. I carefully put it on thinking,

"I must guard you more carefully. I will trust no one with you."

I should have been ecstatic to be home, but oddly enough, I wasn't. I wondered how my dear sweet Ryan was. I missed him already. I didn't know how I would live without his love. When I first Traveled, I had no intention of falling in love, only of finding Duke and then my royal jewels.

Just as I finished that thought, Madeleine escorted two of my other maids into my bath carrying buckets of hot water so she could prepare my bath. Once the other two maids left, I disrobed and got in. It felt so soothing. I lay back in the warm water, relaxing my weary mind and body until awful pounding on the front door interrupted my tranquility. Duke, lying beside the tub, growled. It had to be the cousins! They did not waste a second of time.

I reached for my emerald green robe to cover myself in the tub. Won't they be surprised? I was wearing my title. After all, that scoundrel Minton said it paled next to my naked body. I soon heard loud footsteps as my boudoir door burst open.

Thaddeus and Ernest, my nasty cousins, raced in looking as mad as ever. Madeleine stood in the doorway to my bath trying to stop them, but she was not as strong as they were.

"My lords, the duchess is bathing. Please have some decency and give her privacy."

Ernest snarled as they shoved Madeleine aside. "This will be her last private bath in the manor if she does not show us that necklace."

He peeked his ugly head inside my boudoir. "Where is it, Amelia? We know you're in there and without your necklace no less. A reliable source informed us that your necklace was stolen because of your unquenchable libido. Since you no longer possess the necklace, you as well as your entire staff of servants should leave now while your exit will be trouble-free. Take our advice, wench, leave now before we make your departure difficult to say the least. We don't need the necklace to assume the duchy. Just our birth right now makes us the rightful heirs to Abbington Manor."

Ernest laughed as the two men approached the tub. I decided to take them by complete surprise. I stood up dropping my robe into the bath. Madeleine gasped.

"My lady! Please, you are not decent."

I looked straight into the eyes of those dishonorable men and pointed to my neck. "I've been told the necklace pales against the beauty of my naked body. Tell me, do you agree?"

A look of complete horror came over their angry faces. Not from my nakedness, I was quite sure they didn't even notice once they saw the necklace. The pair grumped about something under their breath before they turned in haste to leave. Thaddeus spoke harshly for both of them as they stood in my bedroom doorway.

"Amelia, we are watching you. If anything should happen to that necklace, we will throw you out on the road like a beggar. Understand?"

I just put my hands on my hips and winked. "Enjoy the view, boys. It shall be your last."

They mumbled more incoherent words I couldn't understand, but their expressions alone made it all worthwhile.

"Sit down. We've seen more than enough. We'll show ourselves out."

They harrumphed off, still mumbling.

Madeleine burst into laughter. "My lady, your actions are scandalous! Those two are gone we all hope, once and for all. Now how about a dry robe and some tea?"

Madeleine fetched a towel and another robe. I dried myself before putting on the other dressing gown. I went back to the drawing room where Madeleine delivered a tray with tea and biscuits. That soothed me but did not remove thoughts of Ryan from my mind.

~ * ~

That next week, I tried to carry on with my usual duties. The manor and grounds needed attention due to my absence. I hoped all this work would take my mind off Ryan, but alas, it did not. A week had passed since my return, and I remained worried sick about him. I feared he would never forgive me for leaving.

I understood why Ryan felt he had to help that scoundrel Minton after I shot him, but odd as it may seem, I didn't hate him for that. His compassion was one of the many reasons I fell in love with him. I thought about him so much, I reached a point where I could not concentrate on anything only on thoughts of him.

A few traveling knights visited the manor in hopes of a romantic tryst like they experienced once before. I instructed Madeleine to send them away. She gave me a puzzled look.

"What shall I tell them, my lady?"

"Tell them I am ill. Tell them I am no longer interested in them, tell them whatever you like, but please get rid of them."

I'm sure my actions worried Madeleine. That was so unlike me. But I realized I wanted only one man to love me and that was Ryan

I wanted to know what he was doing and how he was carrying on.

When I sought her help in finding my necklace, Starr told me something that may be of interest now. She said Alden kept a close watch on me since my parents died. He had the most powerful crystal ball, more powerful than hers. I decided to give Alden a visit to see if he could help me check on Ryan. I called on Madeleine for help.

"Please call for my carriage. I need to speak to Alden."

"Yes, my lady. I'll take care of that straightaway."

Anxious to see Alden, I rushed to dress, finding a light green frock that enhanced the emeralds in my necklace.

My carriage arrived just as I finished. During my short ride, I sat anxious about Ryan all the way through the deep woods until Alden's mushroom shaped cottage came into view. When we stopped, I spotted Alden standing in his herb garden checking his plants. Just seeing my kind old seer gave me strength. Alden had been my family's clairvoyant since before I was born. I remember when, as a young child, my mother called on him whenever I was sick. My head, burning with fever, cooled with just his gentle touch.

Older and thinner now, he looked frail wearing spectacles and sporting a long white beard. Even though he dressed in a plain royal blue cloth robe for gardening, he still wore his necklace, a gold and silver interwoven chain with an amulet in its center. It was a quite curious amulet, at that. It was large, the size of four of my fists, made of clear crystal with a curve in the glass. When he held it up to the light, rays of color streamed from its center

I saw he limped now, needing the assistance of a walking stick.

Alden always had a fatherly way about him, ready and patient to listen to my problems. I believed with all my heart he could help me find out about Ryan, help heal any hurt I caused him, and bring about a reunion. When Alden saw my carriage, he waved and shot a caring smile before he had to steady himself with his walking stick. Approaching my carriage with care, he opened the door and helped me down.

I hugged him straight away before I began to plead for his help.

"Alden, please, I need your guidance. You have been my most trusted confidant since I was a child. Starr advised me you have the ability to locate people. I am desperate hoping to find out what happened to a very special friend."

I wiped a tear from my eye as Alden assured me.

"My dear lady, you know it is my mission to help you in any manner possible. I swore to your parents I would look after you as long as I have breath. Please come inside my home. It has been a very long time since you have visited me here."

He was correct. It had been a long time. The last time I visited Alden's home, I came with my mother when I was ten. My mind has fond memories of that day. My thoughts returned to the present when my seer held his arm out to escort me inside. I took it and together walked toward the unusual cottage. Flowers from his garden edged our path ablaze with vibrant colors of red and yellow in both the petals and their leaves. From the exterior, the cottage appeared the same as I recalled, painted pale blue with a dark gray thatched roof. The old mahogany door still creaked when Alden opened it.

The main room had not changed one bit. The mere sight of his seer's paraphernalia always amazed me. Loads of filled apothecary jars, dried herbs and potions crammed the shelves on his walls. I spied his magic wand in the corner near the hearth.

"Please, Amelia, come over to the table and sit down."

I did as he said, sitting on a stool made from a tall tree trunk.

"I shall return in just a minute. I must clean up from the garden if I

106

am to perform magic."

My seer then left walking into a small adjoining room. He returned dressed in a gold and crimson brocade robe wearing his gold and silver amulet with the crystal center. He looked magical as he pushed a tray on wheels carrying a large clear crystal ball. I could not take my eyes off it, noticing how much larger its globe was than Starr's. Alden lifted the crystal ball placing it on the table in front of me. He spoke in soft tones.

"Amelia, how may I be of help?"

"Alden, can your magic find anyone?"

"Yes, anyone you care about."

"Please, I need you to find out what happened to a kind man I met on both my visits to Starr's. His name is Ryan. Ryan Redstone."

Alden paused.

"Ah yes, I watched in my crystal ball as you and Mr. Redstone sat by the river. You are in love with him, aren't you?"

"Yes. I would prefer not to admit that, but yes he is the one."

Alden wheeled his crystal ball over to the table. He sat down on the stool next to mine and looked into that magnificent crystal ball before waving his thin, frail hands over and around it.

The clarity of the contents soon became foggy until they were impenetrable to the naked eye. He held the crystal center of his amulet in front of both the crystal ball and my eyes. The crystal center was curved, making the view inside the ball more precise, as if I was looking through extra strong monocles.

"Amelia, I cannot do this alone. I need you to close your eyes and think about your Ryan. Think about the last time you saw him. Think about how you felt and where you were. Let these thoughts seep into your mind until you can think about nothing else. Your thoughts will guide the crystal ball."

I closed my eyes and did as he said. I remained in complete trust of Alden's powers. My mind began to relax as my thoughts drifted back to

Ryan. I remained in this state for a few minutes when suddenly I heard a *snap*. It was Alden snapping his fingers.

"Look into the ball, Amelia, look."

I took a timid peek and was amazed at what I saw. As Alden waved his fingers around the ball, the crystal center of his amulet sent streaks of white light clearing the ball's foggy contents. I watched, astonished that I could see Ryan. He did not leave Minton alone after I left. He remained in the store to help that scoundrel with his injury. I could hear his voice.

"9-1-1, what's your emergency?"

"We need help. My name is Ryan Redstone. I am in The Seybold Building where a man has been shot and robbed on the third floor, unit 316. He needs immediate medical attention. Please hurry!"

I watched as my knight in shining armor ripped the sleeve from his shirt to make a bandage for that common thief. The authorities arrived in multiple carriages. Six men exited with guns drawn. They entered the building and ran up the stairs. Waiting for the proper moment, they walked into Minton's place, guns pointed at my love. They addressed Minton rather than Ryan.

"Take it easy, sir. Medical help is just down stairs. I'll radio for them to come up stat. Please if you can, tell us what happened."

Minton winced holding his wound. He's lucky he can still hold it. If I had my way he'd be long gone.

"A woman came into my shop pointing a pistol at me, demanding I give her a valuable and historical necklace. She grabbed it and shot me on her way out."

He then turned to Ryan.

"This man helped me, but I wouldn't be surprised if his help was a ruse to look like he wasn't involved. I'm sure by the way he talked to her that they were in cahoots to steal that multi-million dollar piece of jewelry. He may not have pulled the trigger, but he's just as guilty in my eyes. I trusted that he was legit, representing himself as an appraiser from the Smithsonian. He sure had me fooled. Oh, I hurt."

I gasped at how that low life lied. I should have killed him when I had the chance. Two men with some kind of bed on wheels arrived and started to attend to Minton. As they did, I then watched as my Ryan, who was indeed The Good Samaritan in all of this, displayed a total look of disbelief on his face. He was finally able to answer.

"I am not involved with the theft or robbery in any way. I do work for the Smithsonian. I can provide proof. I was here to purchase the jewels legally. Please, you must believe me."

Soon after Minton's statement, three of the constables put their weapons away to approach my love. One removed a pair of shackles from his pocket and secured Ryan's wrists. The guard behind Ryan spoke, "Okay, buddy. You're coming with us. You are under arrest for conspiring to commit armed grand larceny and attempted murder. You have the right to remain silent …"

He spewed off all these rules to Ryan before helping Ryan stand. One of the other constables turned to Minton.

"Don't worry, Mr. Minton. We got it from here. Just take care of yourself."

The constables then escorted Ryan down the odd cubicle out to their waiting carriage. My Ryan gave the guard escorting him to the carriage the most heartbreaking look before getting in.

"Please don't do this to me. You don't understand, sir. I was just as surprised as Mr. Minton. I had no idea Amelia intended to rob him. I am heartbroken. She was the first woman I could love since I lost my wife. She betrayed me and will ruin a career I worked a lifetime to achieve. If I was guilty, why would I stay and try to help? I'm innocent."

The constable responded, not impressed. "That's not what your friend inside says. Besides, I've been on the job a long time. That's what they all say. Save it for the judge."

I watched him hold Ryan's head before placing him in the backseat of a horseless carriage. He looked out the window. I thought I saw his eyes tear. I'm sure deep in his heart, he now believed he had fallen in love with the wrong woman.

Distraught, I continued to watch Ryan seated alone in the backseat of the carriage speak to the driver. "I don't care what happens to me anymore. My heart is broken. The first woman I could love since I lost my wife betrayed me. My career is in shambles. My only concern now is my dog and if I ever get to see him again."

The driver remained quiet. I heard Ryan speak to him again.

"I never want to see that woman again. She could beg me to come back on hands and knees. I'd just turn and walk away."

Did I really hear him say that? I clutched my necklace around my neck wondering if its wealth was worth the price it took on my life.

I leaned in to look some more. The constables escorted Ryan to the prison like structure with a sign that read "Police Station." Once inside, they walked him to a desk. They put ink on his hands, took his credentials, and flashed a bright light in his face. If that was not enough, they took him to what one called "a holding cell." He went inside only to sit beside the meanest looking thugs I have ever seen. *Oh, my love, what have I done to you?* I watched as Ryan stood and motioned for a guard to come over.

"I would like to make my phone call now, please."

A woman constable escorted Ryan to a black device on the wall not far from his prison cell. Ryan handed the officer a note. She read it before pushing the device's buttons. Soon, I heard a familiar tone. *That was the gypsy's ring!* Ryan spoke under his breath.

"Please be home. I don't want to leave a message."

Ryan breathed a deep sigh of relief when he heard her voice.

"Starr Knight here. How may I help you?"

Ryan spoke quickly, as if afraid he won't get all the information out in enough time.

"Starr, it's Ryan. I have to be very careful describing what just happened. If I even mention what Amelia is capable of doing, they'll just put me in a strait jacket and take me away. I had to call you, Starr. You are the only person on earth who knows the truth. I don't have much time. Amy betrayed me. She wouldn't wait for my help. I didn't know she had a gun. She shot my business contact, stole the necklace, and disappeared into thin air. Now I'm accused of being her accomplice and have been arrested. I need help getting out of jail. If ever I needed your help, it's now. I should have heeded your warning about her. I thought with my heart rather than my head. Please tell me you'll help. I'm in the central Miami police station."

I watched with remorse as the following events unfolded in Alden's crystal ball. By the look on Starr's face, I could see she was surprised.

"Ryan, of course I'll help you, but tell me why didn't you call a lawyer?"

"I can't call a lawyer. I can't have my employer learn of this matter until the whole thing has been cleared up. You are the only contact I trust here. Besides, being so far from Washington, I wouldn't know how to choose a lawyer in Miami. I hope you'll come help me clear my name and tell the police the truth about what happened even though I don't know if they'd believe us."

I heard silence on Starr's end of the conversation. Ryan pleaded.

"Starr. Please, you have to help me. I am in a bad bind. I have never been arrested. I never had anything like this happen to me before. I called you because I can't afford to have any one else know about this."

Starr sighed before speaking. "Ryan, I wrongly assumed you went to Miami alone. Amelia told me she was going shopping. I trusted her and did not check up on her whereabouts. She used you, not to mention me, and will have to pay for that, but at a later time. Please trust me. It may take a couple of days, but I'll help. In the meantime, speak to no one. Tell them you have to wait for council. You have that right."

My Ryan took a deep breath. "Thank you. You know I trust you. I will wait to hear from you no matter how difficult it becomes for me. Please, if I could ask a favor of you. The phone number for the vet where

Stormy boards is on the back of the photo I left with you. Please call and tell him I will be delayed."

Starr's kind voice answered. "I will. Stay strong, Ryan. I will take care of everything."

Ryan stopped talking before handing the device to the constable. She placed it back on the wall before escorting Ryan to his cell. My heart shattered. He looked so forlorn and it was all because of me.

I started to cry and looked up at Alden. "This is entirely my fault. What am I to do?"

Alden gave me a stern look. "Amelia, my child, you will have to make a most difficult choice. I cannot send you back to Ryan nor protect you from Starr's anger. We all are guilty of something we are not proud of doing, but it is how we deal with the consequences that makes us who we are."

Alden held up his crystal amulet again. I looked through its clear rays to see Starr pacing around her reading room. She spoke to herself.

"That dirty little snake. How dare she treat Ryan like this? She and I are going to have a talk."

I have not known Starr long but have never seen her behave in this manner. She stomped around her reading room before taking out her crystal ball. She placed it on the table before waving her hands over it with such intense passion, she nearly fell over. A kaleidoscope of colors soon filled the room. The lights circled her until the haze in the crystal ball cleared.

"Aha. There you are, you trollop. I see that you are with Alden. He cannot protect you from me. Alden forgive my actions, but Amelia has done hurtful things to a good person. I am calling you, Amelia, to come here."

I looked at Alden frightened out of my mind.

"Is that true? Can she do that?"

Alden nodded. "Amelia, Starr has a secret power, one that she rarely employs. She has the ability to call someone back to her time, especially if they betrayed her. Your actions, even though you may think otherwise, did just that. Now, please go gracefully. It is best not to fight these powers."

I was afraid. I didn't intend to hurt Ryan. I loved him. I certainly did not want to disrespect Starr. Trembling, I watched the gypsy hold her hands in the air and wave them around. She closed her eyes speaking words I hoped not to hear.

"Bring the past to me. Bring the past to me. Amelia, Duchess of Abbington, betrayed me. I want her to appear in front of me now!"

Just as soon as I heard Starr finish those words, I felt odd. I looked over at Alden. He removed his crystal amulet from my view to take a few steps back. His face became blurry as my thoughts clouded. My mind and heart were swimming in guilt. My stomach churned. I feared something but was unaware what.

I could hear the faint whooshing sound of the winds as they left Starr's house to enter the atmosphere of time. I held my necklace tight when I heard that eerie sound approach Alden's cottage like a furious storm at sea. How could this be? I did not call her! How dare Starr send these winds for me?

I watched Alden back up and crouch in the corner near his hearth. I was sure that he too could hear those thunderous sounds as they approached. The dark winds swirled around Alden's room before coming to a screeching halt directly in front of me. Why did they stop? I sat down hoping I would be out of reach. Suddenly a large gust started up again. The magnitude of its power picked me up and thrust me into the center of its cyclone. I was in pain, my body ached, never having felt the cruel side of these winds before. I did not panic. I remembered what Alden said. I did not fight them. I spun around until I lost consciousness. Then they came to an abrupt stop. *Crash*! I landed so hard on the floor of the gypsy's reading room, I rolled over and awoke whimpering from pain. I glanced up to see Starr standing over me, hands on her hips. She looked angry ...very angry. I have never seen the kind gypsy like this before. She stared deep into my eyes.

113

"Didn't you think I would find you, you lying witch?"

I didn't respond not knowing what to say.

Starr continued. "All you care about is yourself and that foolish necklace of yours. Ryan is a broken man rotting in jail. He fell in love with you. He trusted you and loved you with all his heart. I said loved. Somehow I don't think he does any longer."

I heard her hurtful words and began to cry. "Starr. I am truly sorry. I had to get my inheritance back. I have staff with families that depend on me. I gave them my word that I would take care of them and had no intention of getting Ryan involved with any of this because I love him."

Starr softened her look a bit. I hoped she could sense I was telling the truth.

"Didn't you realize that just the fact that Ryan was present during your actions makes him an accomplice in the eyes of the law? You left him with a broken heart and a ruined reputation. How can he work in the jewelry appraisal business after being charged with armed grand larceny? That's the highest form of robbery. He's distraught, rotting away in prison while you, you selfish witch, bask in the luxury of your manor house with its servants, gardens, and high tea admiring your necklace daily in the mirror. How could you? I trusted you. Doesn't that count for anything?"

I could not stop crying. "I do love him. My love for him is true. He was not just one of my flings. For the first time in my life, my feelings were real. We are from such different times and places. You know as well as I do that I can't stay in your time for more than seven days. Even if I wanted to remain on a permanent basis, because my problem was resolved, I would become my true age, dust. I should have asked him to come back with me and be my duke. I was too impulsive, too upset about my inheritance. I am so sorry. I will do anything to make it up to him and you. Anything."

"Anything? Really anything? How much do you love him? Would you take your necklace to the police and give it up to clear his name? Tell me Amelia, how much do you really love him?"

114

I sat back. Tears streamed down my cheeks like a torrential rainstorm. *My necklace? Doesn't she understand the necklace is the key to my entire world?* I grasped my necklace as tight as I could. I took a big breath, unclasped it, and placed it on the table. I reluctantly pushed it toward her.

"I will do whatever it takes to make this right for Ryan. I love him more than anything else in the world, including my title and this necklace."

Starr contemplated my actions. "You're sure you want to do this?"

I straightened myself. "Yes, I am sure. Take it. Hurry, before I change my mind."

The gypsy shot me a sympathetic smile. She picked up the necklace and placed it in her bag.

"Good then. Now please go upstairs to freshen up and change. You must appear like you're from this time. Once we arrive, if anyone should speak to you, refrain from mentioning that you are a Traveler. They'll put you in a strait jacket. As soon as you're ready, we'll leave. I'll hold onto your necklace for safe keeping."

I nodded in silence, got up, and went upstairs. No matter how despondent I was about the fate of my duchy, my heart assured me I was doing the right thing for the man I loved.

I could hear Starr speak to someone at the police station. She wanted to find out when and if Ryan could have visitors. She arranged for us to visit later that afternoon, identifying herself as Ryan's legal representative. I'm sure the police took it to mean his barrister. Once refreshed, I went downstairs to let her know I was ready. She grabbed her keys.

"Okay, let's go."

I did not know if I could see him, or if I too would be banished to a cell. I needed answers.

"Will I be able to talk to him?"

"I'm not sure. We'll see when we get there."

I followed Starr to her small horseless carriage. We made the two-hour trip to Miami, speaking very little along the way. Those two hours passed like two days. Once we were in the large city, Starr stopped for directions to the station. We rode there and she found a space for her carriage across the street. She turned.

"Are you prepared emotionally for this? I will try to get you in to see him. If I am successful, you will talk to him first."

To be honest, I didn't know if I was ready. What do you say to the first man who stole your heart after you let him down? I didn't know if I could bear the thought of what he might have to say to me. Apprehensive, I was slow to step out of her buggy and walk with her across the street.

Starr held me by the arm either for support or to prevent me from changing my mind. We entered the station together. It was not anything like I thought. No torches. No dark dungeons. No scary large men wearing black face masks carrying large weapons. Starr advised the gentleman at the front desk who we were and why we were there. At once, another man came to us and escorted us into a clean room with a table and chairs. It even had light. We sat down, waiting minutes that felt like years.

When the door opened, I watched as a large guard brought Ryan in shackled. Ryan saw us seated at the table. His eyes sharply turned away from mine.

"Officer, please take me back to my cell. I don't want to see that charlatan."

He raised both bound arms to point in my direction. As the guard turned him around to leave, Starr jumped up. Her voice begged his attention.

"Ryan, don't turn your back on her. You're much too smart for that. Please just hear her out. Amy has come back to make things right."

Ryan nodded to the constable to let him go back in. He sat down across from us. The gentleman who escorted Ryan looked at Starr.

"Are you his legal representative Starr Knight?"

"Yes sir, I am."

The constable pointed to Ryan's wrists. "Cuffs on or off, ma'am."

She responded without hesitation. "Off, please. He's an innocent man. He won't hurt anybody."

"Okay, then if you're sure. I'll be right outside if either of you ladies need any help."

The constable took the shackles off Ryan.

Starr smiled.

"Thank you, sir. I'm sure we'll be fine."

The constable left closing the door to give us some privacy. Starr waited a few minutes before speaking.

"Ryan, Amy is here to tell you something important. Give her a chance and listen."

My love stared daggers at me. Tears streamed down my face as I looked into Ryan's soulful eyes, hoping to soften his gaze.

"I love you. I love you with all my heart. I had no idea you would be taken prisoner. We are from different times and go by different laws. In my time, if you stayed to help a bleeding victim and had no weapon, you would be considered a hero, but I have since found out not in yours. I came back to set the record straight and prove my love to you."

Ryan shrugged his shoulders and looked away, but he said, "Amy, why would you do this to me? You can't have real feelings for me. I trusted you. You, the first woman I could love since Jillian died, betrayed both my love and trust. What could you possibly do to restore my faith in you, short of giving yourself up and taking the blame, what?"

I sat back. *How will I ever convince him?* I sensed how deep his hurt was. I looked into his blue eyes again before addressing Starr.

"Please show him the necklace."

She took the black velvet bag from her purse, opened it, and placed the necklace on the table. I could see Ryan was taken aback by this. I reached for his hand but he pulled it back.

"Ryan, please, you have to believe me. I am prepared to give my necklace to the authorities. I have come back to clear your name even if I have to give up my inheritance, my freedom, and perhaps my life. You are the only man I have ever loved. Your love is worth more than any necklace. Starr, please take the necklace to the authorities. Tell them I wish to speak to them."

Ryan sat back still stunned by my actions. Starr pushed my necklace over to him. She stood.

"Ryan hold onto this. I'll go get an officer who can help clear your name. Those are Amy's instructions."

Ryan shook his head no. He looked into my eyes. "Amy, don't do this. They'll arrest you. Because of who you are, you'll die a quick death in prison. I want to clear my name but can't bear the thought of doing it that way"

I stood up and walked over to him. "Does that mean you still love me? I hope so. I still love you with all my heart. That is why I came."

Ryan's gaze turned tender. I could see he must have realized I took great risks to come back and help him.

"Amy, I do love you. I love you more than you know. I would rather serve an unfair term in prison than have anything happen to you."

I reached for his hand and got down on my knees. "Ryan, come back to my time with me. I am proposing. Marry me. That is the only way we can stay together for the rest of our lives. You'll be far from idle. You can work with our local jewelers and artisans. I want this more than anything. I will leave the necklace here with the authorities and renounce my duchy. We will live like the other happy commoners in my village. All that I have means little to me without you."

I turned to Starr. "Starr, can you make this happen for us?"

She grinned. "Yes, I can remove the time restraints for Ryan so he can remain in your time for the rest of his life. But you both must be sure, very sure, for he will not be able to return. This cannot be undone. Ryan may even get sick, as Time Travel does have its ups and downs."

Ryan listened but remained quiet. Staring deep into my eyes, he whispered. "Amy, I never expected to see you again. I believed with all my heart that you were using me. If I do go back with you, you must promise that you will be faithful to me and never lie to me again."

My heart raced. My eyes teared. He surprised me! I still have a chance!

"Yes, Ryan. You know I will. I shan't lose you again."

Ryan wanted to be sure. "And you won't betray me again."

"No," I answered. "This was not meant as betrayal. I did not know your laws."

Ryan squeezed my hand as tight as he could. "There's only one problem with this. I'm an old-fashioned guy. I guess I should be the one who does the asking."

He got down on his knees. We were eye to eye. "Will you marry me, my beautiful lady?"

I started to cry with more tears of joy. "Oh yes, Ryan I will."

We both stood and kissed. We kissed for so long Starr had to interrupt us. I glanced over at her. She was smiling from ear to ear. I think she wanted this for us as much as we did, but she gave us a stern warning.

"Both of you have to be certain. I remind you. There is no turning back. I need to hear this from each of you.

Ryan spoke first.

"I love Amy and want to go back with her and remain in her time. I am sure."

Starr then turned her glance to me.

"I want Ryan to come back with me. He is the first man I have ever truly loved. I am very sure but have one question. Shall I leave my inheritance here on the table for the police to find or should you take it to them?"

Ryan looked at the necklace. He picked it up as if pondering my question.

"Amy, this necklace is your birthright. I believe that Minton is the real scoundrel in all of this. Take it with you. You proved your love to me by wanting to leave it here. Minton doesn't deserve to lay claim to your necklace nor the dishonest money he would get from it. Please, let me put it around your neck."

I turned around so he could fasten the clasp just as Starr chimed in.

"I agree with Ryan. You risked a great deal to come here. You should not leave your necklace for that thief only to return home and find your duchy in the hands of your unscrupulous cousins. Now, let's get ready for Travel. We must do this at once so as not to alert the guards. After you leave, I will cast a spell on this station and everyone in it so they do not look for you."

I looked at Starr, wondering what we should do next. She must have read my mind because, before I could ask, she advised us.

"Stand together over there by that wall. Please hold hands. Amelia, make sure your necklace is fastened securely and hold on tight to Ryan. You want to make him a duke, don't you?"

Elated, Ryan and I did what we were told. Starr whispered as she waved her hands in the air several times. The window on the door to the room fogged up as she spoke these words.

"Oh, winds of the past. Take Ryan and Amelia back to Amelia's time. Make it safe for Ryan to remain there for the rest of his life. Winds of the Past. Winds of the Past. Take them back and keep them safe—protect these lovers with all of your mystical powers."

As soon as she finished, all three of us heard the ominous loud whooshing of the wind. The churning air entered through some small holes in the ceiling. It picked the two of us up in its cyclone. Those same small holes expanded into large ones as we passed through them and out into the atmosphere. We spun around, holding on tight to each other like ballroom dancers. Once a safe distance away, we stopped spinning and found ourselves floating in place over the police station. I signaled for Ryan to look down. We could still see and hear the guard knock on the door to the room we had been in.

"Everything all right in there, Ma'am?"

We watched as Starr cleared the fog while remaining in the conference room long enough for us to leave. Unfortunately for us, she couldn't silence the loud whooshing wind and it was heard inside the Miami police station. The constable outside Ryan's door called in to her right after hearing those menacing sounds.

"Hey, everything all right in there or do I have to come inside?"

Starr responded. "Why, yes, it is. Is that a sudden storm I hear brewing outside?"

He yelled back, "Don't know for sure. Could be a no name, I'm sure you know what they're like if you live here. It's one of those sudden intense Florida storms that seems to come out of nowhere. Sure sounds like a whopper heading our way."

As the sounds of the winds become fainter, Starr opened the door a crack and looked out before exiting the room. Once in the hallway, she spoke to that constable so as not to cause suspicion. She noticed he had handcuffs and keys ready to greet Ryan.

"Excuse me sir, I failed to tell you that the young lady you escorted inside is Mr. Redstone's future wife. Please allow them fifteen minutes alone after I leave before taking Mr. Redstone back to his cell. You know young love. They want to talk about their future together. That is, if he has a future."

We watched the constable put his handcuffs and keys back in his pocket. "Okay, as long as I don't hear any strange noises going on."

They shared a laugh. Starr further assured him.

"I'm confident you won't hear a sound. I have instructed them to remain as quiet as possible. Good day sir. Thank you for your help."

With that, Starr strode out of the station to her carriage and got in before moving it out of sight. We held hands, still floating, as that constable waited fifteen minutes before opening the door to the conference room. He gasped. I'm sure our absence took him by complete surprise. The room was empty. He removed the box from his belt.

"Alert. Alert. Redstone escaped with his girlfriend. That guy is a regular Harry Houdini. They can't be far. This door is the only way in or out. Advise all officers. Nobody in or out of the building. Find that lady who claims to be his lawyer and stop her! Have some patrolmen search the grounds and nearby streets."

He put his box back and searched the room for clues as he held his head.

"Where is that lying lawyer of his, anyway? I should have known she was an imposter. How could I be so stupid to fall for her story?"

By that time, Starr had relocated the carriage around the corner. She got out and hid in some very tall bushes.

"I think I'll have a little fun. It's been a difficult day for everyone."

She looked up. "Hope you two love birds can see this. Oh, magic winds, wrap your strong gusts around the police station. Make it impossible for anyone to leave. Wipe clear those policemen's minds and all their paperwork of any memory of Ryan, Amelia, or Starr. Erase. Erase Ryan, Amelia, and Starr from their minds and records. Erase them now."

We looked down at the station. The constables stopped running around looking for an escaped prisoner. They were all back at work.

"Ah. One more detail to make this complete."

Starr closed her eyes again. "Winds of time. Pick Stormy up. Return him to his master. Let Stormy live the rest of his days with Ryan, Amelia, and Duke."

She laughed as she got back in her carriage to drive home. "Oh, I wish I could have seen the look on that officer's face when he found that empty conference room."

Ryan and I kissed before those soft winds blew us back to my time. Our Travel was most genteel. We felt like we were floating on clouds until we slowed down and, with one loud thud, landed in my dressing room. The noise startled Madeleine, who was cleaning in the grand hallway. Duke heard us as well and barked. What's this? We heard a second bark. I heard Madeleine run up the stairs before rushing in. My little Duke followed with Ryan's Stormy at his heels. It took seconds for Stormy and Duke to be all over us, knocking us to the ground and wagging their tails.

Ryan exclaimed. "Stormy, buddy. I thought I'd never see you again. If you can hear me Starr, thank you. Thank you for allowing me to remain with the love of my life and my best friend. I can never repay your kindness."

I was pleased to see Ryan so happy. Odd, I felt like someone else was watching us. Surprised, I saw Alden observing us from a large chair in the corner of the room. He stood and approached us before speaking.

"Ryan, I am sure Starr will hear you. I shall make sure of that. She alerted me to your Travel. Amelia, I am most proud of you."

Madeleine, on the other hand, was not as affected by our happy homecoming. She shook her head in disapproval, pointing to Ryan and myself on the floor wearing unusual clothing.

"My, my lady, where on earth do you find these clothes? They are shameful. And, sir, you are in orange. Alden tells me you are to be our future Duke. Not at all proper attire for a royal. We must do something about this at once."

She turned her scolding to me. "My lady, that is not at all proper attire for a lady of your stature let alone for your gentleman about to

123

become a royal. I'm afraid there will be no messages, Alden, until these two appear properly clothed like the royals they are. And where did this large dog you call Stormy come from? He was found watering my near perfect flower beds. He was so sweet, and Duke liked him so much, I decided to keep him."

Before either of us could answer, Madeleine called for a male servant to help clean and dress Ryan. She took my hand.

"I'll take care of you myself."

We were gone for about thirty minutes. Alden said he would wait for us. When we returned in suitable attire, Alden signaled for us to follow him into the library. My seer then called for one of my guards. Alden whispered instructions to him before my guard left the room. He soon returned, carrying with great care Alden's large crystal ball, and placed it on the long rectangular library table. Alden looked at us.

"Please sit down. We will contact Starr to thank her. Is there anything else I should tell her?"

"Yes. But I need a few more minutes."

I am so grateful that Alden is patient. I stood and went to my desk taking out paper and removing the quill pen from the top. I wrote and showed my note to Ryan before handing it to Alden. Ryan shook his head yes and kissed my forehead.

I handed my seer the note on my personal stationery. "Thank you for waiting. Please send Starr this, as well."

Alden nodded and read the note. He then held his crystal amulet up so both Ryan and I could look through it. As the fog in the crystal cleared, we could see Starr. She looked exhausted. Her head rested on her reading room table. She appeared to be taking a catnap. She sat up, awakened by the tinkling sound of a message in her crystal ball.

"Now, what's this? A message from the past? Oh, how I hope Amelia and Ryan had no difficulty in Travel."

She read my message first. "Ryan and I can never thank you enough for our new life."

Starr watched as a gold leaf envelope with my royal crest appeared in her crystal ball.

"This gold hand lettering inked on beige parchment is from Amelia. It displays the seal of Her Grace, the Duchess of Abbington."

Starr leaned in to get a closer look as the envelope opened in her crystal ball. She saw the note and read it aloud.

"Her Grace, Amelia Augusta Ethrington, Duchess of Abbington, requests the honor of your presence at her marriage to Master Ryan Redstone, next Sunday, the 23rd of May, 1753 at three in the afternoon. The ceremony to be performed by her royal seer Alden with guard dogs Stormy and Duke in attendance and will be held at the Abbington Manor. A reception and high tea will follow in the Manor Gardens."

Starr shot up from her chair and danced with joy. "How wonderful! Another happy couple! Oh, how I wish I could be there." Her thoughts soon changed as she glanced at the clock on the wall. "That late already? Better hurry and get ready for my next appointment."

With that she scampered upstairs hoping to make two new lovers as happy as Ryan and Amelia.

About the author

Ever dream of traveling through time? Mariah Lynne does. She writes stories that take her readers along on exciting journeys. Travel to distant times and beautiful places with strong-willed independent heroines whose memorable tales will entertain with twisted plots that dabble in the paranormal. *Shadows Across Time* fits that description to a T as do her previous works *The Love Gypsy* and now *The Duchess' Necklace*.

A Graduate of Syracuse University, Mariah lives on a beautiful Florida Gulf Coast Island where she has written weekly entertainment columns for two island newspapers. Because she loves where she lives, Southwest Florida takes center stage in her stories.

She is a member of Romance Writers of America and the Southwest Florida Romance Writers who recently published two anthologies: "*From Florida With Love: Sunsets and Happy Endings.*" Mariah's short story "Love At First Flight" is included while "The Kaine Mutiny" is included in *From Florida With Love: Sunrise and Stormy Skies* Her short cozy mystery "Claws For Justice" is featured in *Nine Deadly Lives; An Anthology of Feline Fiction.*

When she is not writing, she enjoys swimming, traveling and spending time with her husband and her dolphin hunting dog, Max. To learn more about Mariah and her Time Travel adventures visit her at:

Website: www.MariahLynne.com
Twitter:@mariahlynne1
E-mail: MariahLynneAuthor@yahoo.com
Facebook:
https://www.facebook.com/pages/MariahLynne/295721153858612

Other Works by the Author with Melange Books, LLC

Shadows Across Time